For Eden—
Stay Fierce!

Prince charming

by

S. CELI

This is a work of fiction. Names, characters, places, brands, media, and incidents are either the product of the author's imagination or are used fictitiously. The author acknowledges the trademarked status and trademark owners of various products referenced in this work of fiction, which have been used without permission. The publication/use of these trademarks is not authorized, associated with, or sponsored by the trademark owners.

http://www.saraceli.com/

Without limiting the rights under copyright reserved above, no part of this publication may be reproduced, stored in or introduced into a retrieval system, or transmitted, in any form, or by any means (electronic, mechanical, photocopying, recording, or otherwise) without the prior written permission of the above copyright owner of this book.

Published by Lowe Interactive Media, LLC
Copyright ©2014, All Rights Reserved by Sara Celi
Cover Design by Mayhem Cover Creations
Cover Photography by Amy Elisabeth Photography
Special Thanks: Artfully Disheveled
Cover Model: Joel Geiman
Formatting by JT Formatting

ISBN-13: 978-1494954444
ISBN-10: 1494954443

First Edition: January 2014
Library of Congress Cataloging-in-Publication Data

Celi, S.
    Prince Charming / S. Celi – 1st ed
    1.   Fiction - Romance   2.   Fiction - New Adult

For anyone who has ever searched for Prince Charming.

Chapter One

TUESDAY, JANUARY 22

AP EUROPEAN HISTORY sucked. So did AP Biology, AP German, and AP English. Even World Cultures class sucked.

Everything about senior year at Heritage High School sucked.

I sat in the second row for every class, and I hated it. It should have been the best year of my life—everyone told me that, but they lied to my face. They looked me straight in the face and lied. By the time we came back from winter break, everything about senior year had turned into a boring mess, like we were all just waiting for the day when we'd walk across the stage in the auditorium and get our diplomas.

I didn't know how to change any of it.

Mr. Langston's AP English class was the suckiest of the suck. Fifth period. Somehow, this sorry excuse for an English teacher managed to warp what should have been my favorite subject into a pathetic placeholder in my schedule that always reminded me just how much I was over high school. I'd been over it for most of my senior year, and I wanted to turn around and leave every time I walked into that class. Of course, I never did. Oh, no. I was too much of a pussy to pull something like that.

Besides, school itself had become too damn easy.

The spring of junior year, I'd loaded up my senior schedule with AP classes, designed to give me dozens of hours of college credit as long as I made fours and fives on the tests in May. The guidance counselors and teachers told me over and over again how great this would make my future—that it would complete my path to the top of Heritage High School's graduating class. I liked being at the top.

No, I *loved* being at the top.

And that's how I wound up in the second row of Mr. Langston's class, right after lunch every day, just in time to smell cafeteria food on his breath while he spouted off highbrow comments about classic literature.

"Can anyone tell me three character archetypes often used in Shakespeare?" he asked as he paced across the classroom the Tuesday after Martin Luther King Day. He wore a long green sweater with large wool pills and flakes of Wheat Thins from his lunch all over his chest. He showed up in that sweater every Tuesday.

I cringed every time I saw it.

No one answered Mr. Langston right away. We might have been a classroom of students bound for college and full-ride scholarships, but that didn't make us eager to answer probing questions from an unmarried man in his forties with two lower teeth missing and small scabs on his face from too many shaves with a blunt razor. In fact, the stalemate between teacher and students had grown more pronounced as the school year inched onward.

"Anyone? Hmm? Anyone?" He held up the thick AP English textbook the school issued us at the beginning of the year to help us study for the AP test in May. His edition lacked a cover, and the front pages curled around the edges. Some of the pages threatened to flap out onto the front row. "This was in the required reading."

Still no one raised a hand. Seconds ticked by on the clock. Any enthusiasm we once had fled the room back in September, when Langston's revised syllabus laid out a long line of torturous classics instead of American literature. Nothing crushed teenage spirit faster than Homer. Nothing. And no, Shakespeare did not help any.

"Come on people, this is not difficult," Langston said, his voice squeaking in a way that screamed annoyed and frustrated. He ran his hand along the bald spot on top of his head. "Character archetypes. Think really hard."

I looked up from the small doodle of a sinking ship I'd drawn on a random page in my notebook and glanced at the rest of the class. My eyes fell on blank faces and bored stares from kids I competed with for the top of class rank. We were the top 20 students in the class, and, at that moment, I ranked an irritating second.

Only one face in the crowd didn't get a glance from me. Glancing might turn into staring, and that wouldn't be okay at all.

I couldn't look at *her*. I'd get a hard-on the size of Texas if I did. It had happened before.

"Geoff," Langston snapped, slapping his book on the side of his desk.

My head snapped in the direction of his voice.

"Geoff Miller. I know you have the answer."

"Huh?"

"The answer to this question, in the required reading. I know you completed the assignment."

Sometimes a sterling reputation with teachers really stunk, even if my hard work had earned me one. In almost twelve years of school, I'd never handed in one late assignment, skipped class, or received lower than an eighty-eight on a test. Now, in the winter of my life at this miserable high school, that reputation followed me from class to class, teacher-to-teacher, as if they all just expected that I would never be anything different, other than the perfect student with every answer.

I blinked at Mr. Langston and contemplated cracking a joke, or answering him with a snappy comeback that would make the rest of my classmates laugh. God knows I'd thought of more than a few during that specific lecture, most of which involved some kind of joke about boobs and Shakespeare loving sex. I even envisioned the looks on my classmates' faces. It would be epic.

But, of course, like a model student, I kept all the smartass comebacks to myself.

"Shakespeare didn't mind using character archetypes," I said after a couple of seconds. "In fact, most of his plays have them."

"Very good, Mr. Miller, but I asked for specific examples."

"The star-crossed lovers, the shrew, the villain."

"Yes, you're right." He threw the book down on his desk and looked satisfied. "I can see at least one of us has done the required reading, and as usual it is Mr. Miller."

I glanced around the room fast enough to see three eye rolls from my fellow classmates, and a blank stare at the chalkboard from the face I tried my hardest to avoid focusing on every day during this class. She never looked at me. She didn't even know I was alive.

To Laine Phillips, I was just a waste of air.

The door to my locker slammed shut about thirty seconds after I opened it. I had just grabbed my AP Bio textbook when it happened.

"What's up, Ge-off."

I swallowed my annoyance. Would it kill him to pronounce my name correctly? Apparently, it would.

"The one and only."

"Whatever, asshole." Blake Smithson folded his muscular arms and the white pleather of his letterman jacket creaked. Various awards for football decorated his chest, including one that reminded everyone of his coveted place on the state championship football team. "You're supposed to give us a ride later."

"I know. Mom told me."

Blake leaned up against my locker, ensuring I wouldn't be able to open it again as long as he stood there. "Don't be late this time. Like, you know, late because you're looking up shit in the library."

"Like, what kind of shit?"

"You know. Academic shit."

"Because all stuff in the library is academic shit."

Blake blinked at me as if I'd spoken in Chinese.

"Why do you have to keep rubbing your brains in my face?"

"That's impossible." I widened my eyes to keep from rolling them.

"Whatever. You think you think you're so damn superior."

That was where he was wrong. I didn't *think* I was intellectually superior to Blake. I *knew* I was. "I won't be late," I added after a moment, deciding not to push the issue any further.

"Well, the last time you were supposed to drive us, you were."

Blake resembled two tomatoes stacked together. He had a round head, ginger-spiked hair, and jarring blue eyes. The bottom half of his body was circular, too, with defined and developed muscles he'd honed during endless workouts for the football team. He played linebacker on the team, and so did his brother Bruce. In fact, Bruce was his twin, and only a mole near Blake's left eyebrow distinguished him from Bruce.

"Like I said," I replied, growing irritated. I really needed to move on from this conversation and walk down the flight of stairs to fifth period biology. "I won't be late."

"Dude, whatever," Blake said. He slammed his fist against the locker for emphasis. "Your bitch of a mom told my dad she's really getting tired of you."

"I'm sure she is. Since she loves spending so much time with David and you guys these days, instead of me." I turned and walked down the hallway without another word to Blake. He was a liar. Always had been. But I couldn't be sure if he'd lied right then.

Yet another reason why it sucked having Blake and

Bruce as stepbrothers.

Over the last two years I'd dreamed more than a hundred thousand times that my mom had never met David, Blake and Bruce's father. I wished she and I still lived in the small house on Rosstown Ave, with the white clapboard and the apple tree in the front yard. I begged God for another chance for us to be a family, but there was no family to go back to at all. My dad had died from cancer the year I turned six.

David Smithson had been Mom's first high school love. He got divorced from Betsy, Blake and Bruce's mother, our freshman year of high school. About ten minutes after the ink dried on the divorce papers, he asked my mom out to dinner. She accepted over the phone in a voice I'd never heard her use before. Of course, just a few weeks later, David and my mom had rekindled their love.

Of course they did.

"Geoff!" My mother called from downstairs. The shrillness of it seemed to touch everything we owned in the mansion on Ammunition Ridge. "Diiiiiiiineeeeerr!"

"Coming, Mom," I called down the stairs. My voice came out in breathy heaves, because every afternoon since October I'd done fifty burpees and forty-five jumping jacks in my room before allowing myself to check social media. In January, I added one hundred sit-ups three times a week, all part of a private wish that I'd wake up one day in a different body.

Before I left my room, I clicked out of Facebook and

locked my computer. Then I checked it twice. I'd made that mistake before, and I wouldn't again. I didn't want Blake and Bruce posting on my behalf for the third time in three months.

The wide, winding staircase led to the open-air gourmet kitchen, where a variety of smells greeted me: onions, grease, and something sugary. Mom must have been at it again, trying her best to cook the perfect meal. She placed a sizable pot roast with a burned salt crust on the table in the breakfast nook before she turned to me. Blake, Bruce and David already sat in their seats, and the distinctive wide eyes they all shared bulged as they waited for me to take a seat.

"Milk or water?" she asked as she wiped her hands on her black apron. It said "Kiss the Cook" in red stencil letters embellished with red lip prints on the front.

I yanked my chair out from the table and took a seat. The chair scraped the tile floor, and I stifled a grin when I heard it.

David loved to brag. More than once, I'd heard my stepfather tell people he wanted to impress that the kitchen floor had special tiles from Italy he'd found on a business trip five years ago. Each tile cost $150. He made sure people heard the cost when he told the story.

"I'll have water, Mom."

"Good, that's already on the table." She turned her attention to David, who was poised to take a cut from the roast. He'd even already raised his fork. "David, honey, would you like a beer? Maybe something else? A bourbon? Or can I bring up something from the wine cellar?"

I frowned. She always sounded so sugary and submissive when she talked to David. She'd never been that way with Dad. Why was she always changing herself to suit what she "thought David wanted"?

"Sure, sugar," he said. Then he cut into the roast with gusto, clinking and banging the knife and fork as juices spilled out on the white china plate. "Red."

Meanwhile, I resisted the urge to throw up. I hated the way his voice sounded when he said "sugar." It reminded me of the way a drunken cartoon character might speak.

"Pinot?" She picked up a dark bottle with a fancy label from the counter, and held it out like a trophy.

"Yep, sugar, that will work." He didn't even look at her. I wondered if he noticed how much time and effort she'd put into her hair, or the fact that she now wore makeup every evening to dinner. She never used to do that, either. It might have made her look refreshed and polished, but I didn't like it. Not at all.

Blake and Bruce tore into the roast after their dad cut his portion. They didn't acknowledge anyone, they just did it. As my mother and I waited for them to finish, I swirled my fork around the spinach, lettuce, celery, mozzarella, and tomato salad that took up half my plate. Mom had covered the whole thing in a purple dressing, a recipe that I suspected she got from one of the new cookbooks that lined the shelf above the stove. Again, another effort by her to please David. She never cooked very much before she married him.

"Hey, now. Don't play with your food, Geoff," David said once he noticed what I was doing. He added a disapproving arch of his eyebrow.

"What?" I said, incredulous as I looked from my food to David, and back again. "I wasn't playing with it. I was just mixing the dressing." I looked at my mom for reinforcement on this, but she just shrugged.

"Stop mixing the dressing, Geoff," David said. "Eat. Now."

I turned my head to him, taking in the sight of this fifty-year-old man with a comb over, who wore a wrinkled brown suit and red tie. What did my mom see in him? He must have been gangbusters in bed. Or, maybe it was the money. She did have an AmEx with a $50,000 limit now, and a personal shopper at Nordstrom. Access like that must have made up for everything.

I set my fork down against the plate. "What? I'm not playing with my food."

He cleared his throat. "Just eat your food, Geoff."

"But I wasn't—"

"It doesn't matter what you tell me, son. What matters is what I saw."

"I'm not your son."

"I saw you playing with it, Geoff. End of story." He talked with his mouth full of food, and with each word a mix of salad bits and shreds of roast threatened to spray across the mahogany table.

"I wasn't."

"It doesn't matter." My mom sighed. "Eat the roast. It's good." She added a fake smile and pointed at her handiwork. A small piece of beef the size of a dollar bill remained. Mom hadn't eaten any, yet either. Without another word, I cut it in half and left the rest for her.

Chapter two

THURSDAY, JANUARY 24

SENIOR YEAR, I had one best friend: Josh Anderson. We sat at a lunch table with two other guys—Mark Crawford and Nathan Priest—both of whom I called good friends, too. Together, we navigated the choppy waters of the Heritage High School cafeteria, a place where students jockeyed for tables with the best view of the room and ate calorie-balanced lunches made by two chefs the student alumni association paid for with private donations. Of all the dangerous places in the preppy school we called home, the lunchroom was the most dangerous. Student reputations rose and fell by the events in that large, loud room located in the center of the building. What happened in the lunchroom never stayed in the lunchroom, and the social hierarchy of Heritage ebbed and flowed just from that fact, and exactly the way the popular kids liked it.

The four of us ate lunch most days at a spot in the far right corner of the room. The rectangular table sat far enough away from the lunch line to see most of the action, but close enough to check out the hot senior and junior girls. Our section of the lunchroom sat six people, but two of the chairs always stayed empty. Always.

No girls ever sat with us at lunch, despite Mark's best efforts to convince them. Mark crushed on at least five girls during senior year, but he had no skills. Every time he talked to girls, they just wound up laughing in his face. He didn't lose hope, though, and at least once a day he brought up his latest crush.

Nathan, on the other hand, was more interested in his latest level achievement on the *Mass Effect* video game. He'd turned eighteen without having even kissed a girl. Josh, meanwhile, often kept his feelings about girls and the rest of high school to himself.

I think that's why we became such close friends.

"Dude, check out the shirt Jillian James is wearing," Mark said at lunch one typical Thursday. He clutched his burger in one hand, and stopped it a few inches from his mouth as his eyes widened. Lettuce and tomato threatened to fall out of the bun and land on his shirt, but he ignored it. "That sweater is see-through. You can see her tits."

"Tits." Nathan's eyes scrunched up behind his horn-rimmed glasses as he laughed. "You said tits. Such a great word. God, I love that word."

"Even better when they're up close," I said under my breath.

"This is awesome." Mark's eyes followed Jillian as she walked across the lunchroom. "It's like she doesn't even realize people can see them . . ."

I glanced at Josh, then turned my head to see exactly what about Jillian had so distracted Mark from his food.

On that day, Jillian wore a knee-length black sweater over grey leggings. The loose knit of the sweater revealed what looked like a tan camisole underneath, one that hugged her hourglass body. Her long, curly black hair tumbled down her back, and she walked across the lunchroom like it was her own personal runway. A couple of kids stopped eating as she passed. But that didn't mean I could see her boobs.

"Well. I don't see anything," I said.

"You must have missed it, you idiot," Nathan said. "They were out. It's that sweater."

"They were not out. She wouldn't do it, anyway. She's not that stupid." I paused. "Well, she is dumb. But that doesn't mean you saw them."

"You didn't see her from the front." Nathan sounded annoyed. In fact, he sounded that way a lot when he talked to me.

My eyes stayed on Jillian as she made her way to the usual table where she sat. She reached it, placed her tray down, and I sucked in my breath a little bit. She sat right next to Laine, in the middle of the table, and Monica, a brunette, sat across from them. Even though I already knew they were all lifelong friends who sat at the same lunch table every day at Heritage, my heart still jumped from my chest to my ears.

Something about Laine did that to me every time, and not just because she had a rail-thin body and wavy blonde hair.

On that day, she looked perfect in a black turtleneck sweater and fur vest. As I watched, Laine smiled at Jillian, and then said something to her, and they booth laughed. Monica, always the wannabe, laughed, about half a second later.

People were always like that around Laine. She never went long without finding something funny, and her round, warm laugh often made other people laugh, too. She radiated happiness, confidence, and perfection.

The whole scene intoxicated me.

"Nice," Josh said when he noticed what and who had my attention. "Good to see some things never change, including your worship of the princess."

"Shut up. I am not worshiping her."

"So, you do still like her?" Josh's left eyebrow shot up.

"No. I don't—no."

"Whatever." He grinned. "You could run a Facebook page about how much you like her."

"Come on. Shut up."

"She really is a princess. I heard her say something in the hall about how she and Evan went to some concert downtown over the weekend." He shook his head. "Of course she had front-row seats. Snobby bitch."

I glared at him. "She's not a snobby bitch."

"I'm just trying to be a good friend here."

"Yeah, I get that." I didn't hide my sarcasm, because I just wanted Josh to stop talking about her.

"You can look all you want." Josh cleared his throat and pointed his fork at me. "Laine will never look back at you, Geoff. She'll never pay attention to anyone but Evan Carpenter."

Ah, Evan. Damn him.

Also a senior, Evan Carpenter threw for over two thousand yards during the football season that year, and he led the team a 35–14 win over the Bowling Green High School Purples in the state championship game. For the last two weeks, he'd worn a variety of Ohio State jerseys and sweatshirts to school because he planned to play football there in the fall. I only noticed this because he sat in front of me in World Cultures, and he farted a lot. I got to smell it. Right after lunch.

No one at Heritage ever challenged or confronted Evan. The kids at school just idolized him. The class even voted him Mr. Perfect in our junior year.

"She's super-hot though," Mark said his eyes still on her. "I'd take that. If anyone is fuckable celebrity status in this school, it's Laine."

My next bite of food stopped about an inch away from my mouth. "Fuckable celebrity status?"

"Yep. Fuckable celebrity status. But I'd still take Jillian," Mark said, still sneaking glances at Jillian and her huge boobs.

"You'd take anything," I pointed out, but my eyes remained on that table, too. Laine took a bite of her salad. She ate salads a lot. She also only drank water, and on Wednesday, she often bought soup from the hot bar on the far side of the cafeteria. I knew these things because I watched her a lot during lunchtime, more than I wanted to admit to any of my friends.

"I would not just take anything," Mark replied, and then he shook his head and turned back to his wilted lunch. "Laine's one of those girls who will always have everything. But I think Jillian might be more accessible. Maybe even hotter."

"Maybe not. She used to have that uni-brow, and all that acne," I said. "Remember freshman year? Jillian wasn't hot then."

"Plus she's stupid," Nathan said. "She asked me if I

knew the capital of England last week."

"She did?" Mark's lips twisted into a smile he couldn't hide.

"Yep." Nathan smirked. "She didn't know if it was Berlin or Birmingham."

We all laughed. We might not have had girlfriends, but at least we didn't have dumb ones.

A long time ago, the library at Heritage High had hundreds of books spread across two floors. It opened at seven-thirty a.m. and didn't close until four, thereby ensuring nerdy kids like me had a place to hide from the bullies and awkwardness of high school. And we used it for that almost every day.

But not in my senior year. The comfortable library disappeared.

By that time, thousands of dollars in private donations from the parents of Heritage High students paid for a million-dollar renovation to the library. After a summer of construction, the library reopened with only half the physical books it used to contain. They expanded the computer lab, ordered dozens of Kindles, stocked a database full of e-books, and got rid of the card catalog. Heritage High now had the library of the future. I hated it.

Hated it.

I wasn't the kind of person to always embrace change. Change sucked. Change only brought uncertainty, and sometimes that felt worse than the annoyance of mediocrity. But it was still the only place on campus where I could go to avoid the social pitfalls of my snobby high school.

I had a ten-page paper due the following Monday in AP European History on England's Glorious Revolution. Since I hadn't started on it yet, I decided to go to the library that Thursday afternoon.

When I walked in the doors, three other kids sat at rectangular wooden tables spread out in the center of the main library space. Two were freshman, and one was a sophomore. I didn't know any of their names, but I wouldn't have been surprised if they knew mine.

Over the last few years, a couple of epic falls, a science lab experiment gone wrong, and some bad T-shirt choices had cemented my reputation as "Geoff Megadeth," and most of the kids in every grade at Heritage thought they knew all about me.

At least I had that going for my life.

Once I found a seat at one of the wide tables in the far corner, I opened up my binder for the class. My notes filled up 80 percent of the space in the binder, and we still had four more months of instruction before the big test—a test I dreaded, but knew I'd make at least a four on, and a four meant three hours of guaranteed college credit.

Flipping to the back, I found a few blank pages of loose-leaf paper before I slid my school issued iPad out of my backpack. Once I turned the device on, I opened up the McGraw Hill AP European History app and sighed so loudly that one of the freshman a few tables over turned his head in my direction.

"What are you looking at?" I asked, in my most intimidating voice.

His eyes widened, and he lowered his head. Satisfied,

I turned back to my notebook and let the words of a study outline blur together on the iPad. I liked history a lot, but I didn't find England's seventeenth century very interesting, and the thought of creating the required outline before I wrote the paper bored me even more. Why did AP classes at Heritage have so many guidelines? Couldn't they just let us study the topic on our own, take the test, and go home?

"Have you started on your paper yet?" Fifteen minutes later, a voice spoke from behind my left shoulder.

I jumped back in my chair and turned around. What I saw made me catch my breath. Laine stood right next to me, in the flesh. Her letterman jacket threatened to fall off her shoulders, and all the awards, patches, and pins of a celebrated high school career centered on cheerleading leered at me. She hooked her black leather backpack over one shoulder, smiled at me,

"Hey, Geoff."

My ears waited to hear two others words, and when they didn't, my heart fell to my feet. She actually called my name real name—not the stupid nickname? What kind of bizarre world had I fallen into? Maybe I'd wake up in a couple of seconds. Yeah, that's what needed to happen. I needed to wake up from whatever dream this was before it turned into a nightmare.

"Hey, Laine,"

"You look really into it."

"What? No. Yes. Into it. Yummy." I couldn't collect my thoughts. They rattled around in my brain like marbles, and rolled away from me when I tried to string a few together. "I mean, yeah. I'm into tit—I'm into it."

"So you're studying."

"Yeah," I still struggled to talk. "Just working on a

couple of things."

"Have you started on the actual paper yet?"

"The paper?"

"The one for English." She paused. "Mr. Langston's class? The one that's due next week?"

"Oh, that one?"

She smiled. "That one."

"Um . . . no." I closed the textbook, and nodded at the chair across from me. "Do . . . you have a . . . you want to sit down?"

"Sure." She bit her cherry-red lip, and watching her do it almost made me fall out of the chair. Still, she made no move to take a seat. "I wasn't going to come over and talk to you—but, well, I just wanted to say that—well," she broke off. "Never mind."

"Seriously, do you want to sit down?" I asked again.

"Yeah." She looked over her shoulder. "I just don't want to be alone right now."

As I hurried to move my school stuff out of the way, she slid into the metal chair and tossed her own book bag on the floor. Then I just stared at her, because I didn't know what to say, and I couldn't figure out why she'd sat down next to me. It just didn't make much sense. The library had plenty of open tables, and even more computer desks. Hell, she could have had a whole section to herself if she wanted it.

So why me? Why me? WHY ME?

"Have you started the paper?" I asked when the awkwardness became too much for me to bear.

She nodded. "Yeah, last week. I'm about three quarters of the way done with the outline."

"Really?"

"Yeah. I like English literature a lot, especially that time period."

I sat back, surprised. No one liked Langston's class. No one. Right? And she didn't seem like the English type, since she never talked much in that class. I had assumed she got in just because of who she was in school and the magic spell she seemed to have over everyone—even the teachers. "So, you're telling me you like AP English?"

She gave me a blank look, as if I shouldn't be surprised about this.

"Well, that's awesome. I can't get into it. At least, not that stuff we're learning right now."

"It's not that bad, Geoff. Some of it is kinda romantic." She disappeared underneath the table and came back a few seconds later with a thick green binder, a blue pen, and her own iPad. She opened up the binder and pulled the iPad out of the case as a small smirk danced on her face.

"Wait. Are you going to study here?" I paused. "With me?"

"Sure I am. This is a library." Laine winked. "You do know how these work, right?"

"But I mean—"

"And you look so—I don't know—lonely sitting here all alone."

"So you just thought you'd plop down and study with me?"

"What? Don't you want me to?" She tilted her head and frowned, as if she didn't understand why I'd asked the question. "That's what people do in a library. They study. Sometimes together. Of course, I could always go study with one of the freshmen."

But even as she said this, she made no move to get up

from the table we shared. Meanwhile, all the attention in the room had turned to her. Everyone in the library stared, transfixed. She was like that ring from *The Lord of the Rings*. My precious.

Good fucking grief. Of course I would make that kind of lame analogy.

"So, what's the topic you are focusing the paper on?" she asked, as if she had no idea that she had this kind of effect on others. I gulped, and tried to think of an answer. When I didn't get one out fast enough, she pressed onward. "I got the assignment to write about Lady Macbeth as an evil archetype."

"Hamlet," I croaked. "I'm supposed to discuss the psychology of his character."

She looked up from her iPad. "Hmm. That's a pretty easy topic."

"There's just so much to write about. I've been trying to figure out how I can fit it all into a ten page paper." I pretended to sound interested in this—not easy to do when a goddess who looked like the Sugar Plum Fairy had just sat down across from me. I wondered if she tasted as sweet as she looked.

She probably did.

"I hate how we have to turn in all the work, too. I'd rather just write the paper."

"I don't like making the outlines, either," I replied.

"But I like the books on the reading list," Laine confided in a low voice. "My favorite was *The Illiad*."

"Mine too," I lied.

Who was I kidding here? What the hell was I saying?

Laine nodded, as if satisfied with my answer, and turned her attention to the iPad. I seized the further chance to study her up close. She had pulled her hair into a long braid since lunch, and it fell over one shoulder. A few strands of hair escaped, and they danced along her hairline. Close up, her skin looked almost translucent, even though I saw a faint outline of makeup along her chin. My eyes fell on her long lashes—some of which clumped together from too much mascara—her rosebud lips, and the small pearl earrings in her ears.

God, she was gorgeous. More than gorgeous. A gorgeous goddess.

How many times could I think that over and over in my head?

We studied in silence for a while, and the only sound I heard was the click of the large clock on the far wall of the library near the computers. Even the freshmen turned their attention back to their work.

I focused on the notes about England's Glorious Revolution from the iPad app, and managed to create half my outline. Before we knew it, Mrs. McGhee, the librarian, came over the loud speaker to let us know the library would close in five minutes.

Goddamn it.

"Well," I said as we packed up our bags, "I got some work done."

She smiled. "Me too. Good job. Maybe I'll get an A on this paper."

"An A?" I almost dropped my iPad on the floor. "I...um...I didn't know you liked school so much. Guess I'm surprised."

She chuckled. "Of course I like school. I'm in those AP classes with you, you know."

"No, I just—some people don't always like—"

"What? You think I'm just some dumb blonde because I'm a cheerleader?"

"Well—no—" I struggled with a way to fix this, cursing myself inside for saying that. "I just didn't—"

She held up her hand. "Let's clear this up right now. I like AP English, European History, and Chemistry, too. Shock you?"

"Well, yeah . . ."

"You're kinda judgmental, aren't you?"

"Are you trying to psychoanalyze me?" I said, with a fake laugh.

"I don't think I have to. I think I've figured you out." She raised her index finger. "You have a judgmental side."

"I am not. I am not judgmental."

"Whatever."

"I'm not. No, really—"

"I'm ranked fifteenth in the class," she mumbled, as she stood up and zipped her bag. "Of course, that's nothing compared to being ranked second. So I can understand why you might think I was kinda dumb."

"Very funny."

"I'm going to Xavier in the fall," she said. "I haven't told anyone."

"Why not?"

"All my friends think I'm going down to Lexington and UK. Monica even thinks we're going through sorority rush together. But I don't want to do that. Just want to do something different. Know what I mean?"

"Yeah, I do."

I thought about my own early acceptance letter to UVA. I couldn't wait to leave Greater Cincinnati for Charlottesville. Best of all, Blake and Bruce wouldn't follow me. They planned to go to Bluegrass Community and Technical College for two years, and then transfer to the University of Kentucky—if they didn't get D averages.

Losers.

We slid our backpacks around our shoulders and strolled out of the library. From there, it was just a short walk to the front of the school. I didn't have the car that day, so I planned on walking home, and had about a twenty-minute trek ahead of me.

"Are you walking home, or driving?" Laine asked once we stepped out of the school building and into the dreary January day. Cold wind whipped around out faces, and I shuddered inside my navy wool pea coat.

"Walking."

She narrowed her eyes. "Really? You don't have a car?"

"Not today." I shrugged. "Sometimes I like walking. It's not too far."

"No one walks."

"Sometimes I do."

"Whatever." She took a few steps down the sidewalk. "Come on. I'll drive you."

"No—you really don't have to."

"Don't be stupid, Geoff." She motioned for me to come along with her hand.

"Well, what about—"

"Just as long as you don't judge my car," she said with a smile. "People always make fun of me because my parents didn't get me a new one when I turned sixteen."

"People make fun of you?"

She nodded. "Yep. Sometimes they do."

PRINCE CHARMING

"I live in the third house on the left," I said, as we turned onto Ammunition Ridge, a long cul-de-sac in the north end of Robert Hill. The drive home took us past a couple of old churches, a small northern business district with a coffee shop, salon, and convenience store, and streets where the homes got larger with each block. Robert Hill city officials painted the tag line "Scenic City" wherever they could in town, never hesitating to drive home the fact that the town's high taxes and stringent building codes kept the city looking more beautiful than any of the other suburbs that clustered close to Cincinnati. The ease of wealth shone in Robert Hill. Every house had a manicured green lawn, and most featured a garden or landscaped porch. Even, clean sidewalks complimented street medians that doubled as gardens. Local magazines often photographed homes in Robert Hill, and one house near Heritage High had landed a spread in *Midwest Living* back in 2003.

But none of that compared to glittering sophistication of Ammunition Ridge. Behind an iron entrance gate, this street had some of the largest homes in Robert Hill. Ours was a five thousand-square foot Tudor that blended right in with the others, except for the fact that it was the first home built on the street, back in 1950. A four-car garage, washed brick walkway, pool house, and unnaturally green lawn treated with special chemicals, and manicured rose bushes completed the picture. Homeowners on Ammunition Ridge threw parties all the time, and each house contributed HOA fees for an exclusive pool and clubhouse just for residents of the street. Wealth lived there, and no one wanted anyone to forget it.

For ten years, David had lived there with Blake and Bruce, and the three of them refused to move when David married Mom. The twins didn't want to leave their fortress in the furnished basement, which included two rooms, a bathroom, games room, and a separate entrance. David insisted the home had more than enough room for all of us, and he sold Mom on that right after they got engaged. She even got a budget to redecorate the house as she desired, and for the most part I think the home made her happy. She certainly seemed to like her large walk-in closet with a separate alcove for shoes, and the master suite that took up its own wing of the first floor.

Meanwhile, I lived on the refurbished second floor of the house, just off the stairs. Mom and David almost never came upstairs, and the twins only ventured up there if they wanted to annoy me. My room and its adjoining bathroom were far enough away from the noise of the house that I didn't have to hear my stepbrothers talk about stupid stuff, like how much back acne they had from football workouts, or how much money they'd won from bets with classmates about how much pizza they could eat in ten minutes at lunch.

"Wait. This is your house?" Laine said, as she pulled her Toyota RAV4 up to the curb in front of the house. Hearing her obvious awe made me embarrassed. I hated it when David's wealth impressed people. He had so much money, way more than even the standard rich guy, and it came from a mix of old family money and a successful law practice in one of the glass-encased buildings that dotted the skyline of downtown Cincinnati. He had clients like

Proctor & Gamble and KAO. I wondered if he treated them the same way he treated me—with a careful disdain that told me I'd never measure up to his impossible standards.

"Nice place," Laine said.

"Don't you live in something similar?"

Her laughter filled up the car as my face twisted. I could have cut off my lips for asking that. No, I *should* have cut off my lips for asking that. Way to sound like some kind of crazy stalker. Goddamn Facebook, and all its worthless information. We weren't friends on the site, but that didn't matter. I found out plenty about her anyway, just from all the photos people tagged her in to prove they knew her. Even the geekiest and most socially unacceptable classmates of mine wanted to show the social media world they knew her.

"My parent's house is big, but not that big."

"The outside is nothing. You should see the inside. Looks like a decorator vomited in it."

"That bad, huh?"

"Lots of gold and dark wood." I shrugged. "Supposed to give an English hunting lodge vibe."

"Sounds awesome."

My eyes shifted in the direction of the monstrous mansion. "You play your cards right, you just might get to see it." I turned my head back to her and raised an eyebrow. "I overhead Blake and Bruce talking about hosting a party in their basement soon."

"Their basement?" She flipped the SUV's gears into park.

"Yep. They live in the basement, and they have all of it." I leaned forward in case she didn't quite get what I had said. "All. Of. It."

"Nice. Do you have a wing in that place?"

"Just my room." I paused, knowing I had to be careful with my tone. "And I like it there. I do."

"Really?"

"Yeah, I do."

"Are you sure?"

"I do," I insisted. "I like it."

She gave me one of those looks that told me she didn't believe me, but she didn't press me, either. Instead, she shifted the focus of the conversation. "A party? You think you'll be there?"

"Why would I be?" I shrugged. Didn't everyone at school know that while the twins were my stepbrothers, they weren't my friends?

"Might be fun . . ." She trailed off, and for a moment all I heard was the quiet wail of the Dave Matthews Band. She must have liked them. We'd heard their music on the drive home, and I knew I'd never listen to any of their songs the same way again.

I shrugged it off, and tried to stay centered. "I doubt they'd want me there, Laine."

"They might."

"Oh, trust me, I know Blake and Bruce. They don't."

I studied her for another second, taking in the way the car window shined light on her face. God, I had to get out of that car. Fast. Before I did something I'd regret, like shove my tongue down her throat, and then moan her name six thousand times.

"I'm sure they'll invite you. And Evan."

She cocked her head, and her eyes held mine, but she didn't look excited to hear his name. "Evan."

"Your boyfriend? You know, the one who eats whole trays of cafeteria pizza?"

Evan weighed at least 250 pounds, and was the size of three freshmen. The coaches had to order special pads for his football uniform. Facebook told me that, too. So did the *Cincinnati Enquirer*, in its annual write up about our school's illustrious football program. People kept track of these kinds of meaningless statistics about Evan. Almost everyone in town also knew his favorite restaurant (Pete's Grill), his shoe size (13D), and his hero (Tom Brady).

"Right." She turned her eyes away from me, and looked at the street. It was still covered in salt from the recent snow. "Evan." Her eyes floated to the clock on the center dashboard, and the blood rushed out of her cheeks. "Oh God. Look at the time. I should go."

"I didn't mean—"

"Shit."

"Shit? What's going on?"

"I'm late." Her abrupt rely chapped me like the winter wind. "I can't be late."

I know an exit when I hear one, though, and I decided to not press her.

"Thanks for the ride, Laine." I loved the way my tongue felt when I said her name. What I wouldn't give to just get to say it over and over again without anyone thinking I was crazy. I pulled the door handle and hopped out of the car. "Have fun writing about Lady Macbeth."

"I'm sure your paper on Hamlet will be better." She grinned at me, but it looked halfhearted and hurried, as if my presence suddenly annoyed her.

I shut the door and she pulled the RAV4 away from the curb without another glance my way.

Chapter three

FRIDAY, FEBRUARY 1

LAINE HAD SMILED at me every day after that afternoon in the library. Every time she did, it was like I'd stolen a piece of heaven. And every day, I wanted more. So much more.

I'd walk past her between third and fourth period in the hustle between class changes, somewhere between the stairwell entrance and the first landing that led to the math hallway. I had Calculus third period and World Cultures fourth. I used to hate that hallway because it smelled like rotten socks, but I walked it every day senior year because it took me past her.

And since that day in the library, she'd noticed I was there.

She would always give me a large smile, and a nod. Sometimes she'd pause for breath if I caught her on the stairs, but we'd never speak. She'd never stop, and I didn't, either. I knew that right after she saw me, she encountered Evan every day, too. Of course I knew, because I had watched her for so many months, stealing glances in her direction, and looking over my shoulder when I knew something had distracted her.

I lived for that walk. My steps were always lighter and more confident after I saw her. Our eyes would meet, she'd toss me a smile and a lingering glance, I'd smile back, and then we'd both move on to whatever awaited us. And every day that this happened was better than the last one.

Then, one day, she reached out and stopped me on the landing.

"Geoff." She pulled me over on the landing, but our bodies still constricted the space and interrupted the flow of traffic in the hallway.

"Hey, Laine." My toes curled in my shoes, and I had to hold myself back from throwing her against the wall and kissing her right then. Just hearing her say my name sent me to another planet.

"Are you having a good day?"

"Sure I am," I lied. Already that day I had tripped over a shoelace walking to third period, been called "Geoff Megadeth" by some brainless stoner in front of a teacher who didn't do anything, and received only an 80 percent on my Calculus test—a first.

"So, I have a quick question." She bit her lip, which she'd glossed in some kind of bright pink goop.

"Shoot."

Whatever happened next, I wanted this conversation to last forever. I was well aware of all the passing stares we were getting from the rest of the students in the hallway, their looks directed mostly at me in a mixture of confusion and envy. I enjoyed that. Let them look. I had her attention. Me. Not them. Me.

"Are you going tonight?"

"To what?" I feigned ignorance, only to let the conversation drag out.

"To the party later." She laughed, and pulled herself closer to me. I inhaled a combination of floral perfume, bubblegum lip-gloss, and salty lunchroom grease. Absolute heaven.

Times ten.

"Oh, right." I shook my head. "No. I have other plans."

I didn't add that I planned to head to Mark's house for a four-way *World of Warcraft* tournament between the two of us, Josh and Nathan. Nathan said he'd even bring over his dad's vodka, which had sat untouched in his family's liquor cabinet as a casualty of his parent's divorce. This plan sounded more fun than making an appearance as the comic relief at Blake and Bruce's stoner party in the basement of David's house.

"Oh." Her face fell. "It sounds like it's going to be fun."

"I'm not invited."

"Whatever. Of course you are. Aren't your parents out of town?"

"They are. Gatlinburg." I could have rolled my eyes, but I didn't. I didn't want to look too judgmental about David and my mom's clichéd choice for a weekend getaway. Even David's rental of a five-star chalet couldn't take away the tourist trap feeling I got whenever I thought about the one time I went to Gatlinburg during the summer after tenth grade. Still, most of my classmates vacationed in that town, and I didn't want to offend Laine if she liked going there, too.

"How long are they going to be there?"

"Till Monday."

The crowd in the hallway thinned until only a few students walked by us, a signal that the five-minute time change between classes was almost over. It was not the first time in my life that I wished I had Superman powers. It would have been nice to stop time, amongst other things.

"Well, I think I'm going to the party. Evan says he wants to go."

"Ah. Evan. You remember him this time."

She lifted her chin. "Remember him? What are you talking about? Of course I remember him."

"Right . . . um . . . well, that time in the car . . ."

"Oh yeah. That time in the car."

She shoved her sweater sleeves up her arms, and I saw it: an unmistakable yellow, purple and dark blue bruise wrapped around her forearm. What had done that to her? How long had it been there? I couldn't look away if I wanted to, because of its sheer size, and its menacing colors. My expression must have said as much, because seconds after she'd pulled up her sleeves she pulled them down again.

"So. The party," she said, in an obvious attempt to distract me.

"What happened?" I asked. "How'd you get that mark?"

She hesitated and took a step backward. "Anyway. Yeah. So. I guess maybe I'll see you later?"

"But what about the—"

"At the party? Maybe you'll be there?"

"Yeah, maybe. I don't know," I replied, as disappointment and confusion started to creep through my toes and make its way up my legs. "Later."

Then she turned, and bounded down the steps. I stood on the landing and watched her disappear. I didn't move until the bell sounded, and I knew I was late to class for the first time in almost twelve years of school.

I sat on Mark's checkered blue bedspread and stared at the flat screen TV hanging across the room on his wall. Months before, he'd yanked $3,000 out of his summer job savings account and spent it on upgrades and contraptions he found on eBay and Amazon, not stopping until he had two gaming systems, a crate full of accessories, and enough wires to transform his entire wall into a nerd's wet dream. He called it The Wall, and the whole setup looked awesome. I had to admit that.

"Get it . . . what are you . . . this . . . I've got this . . . yes . . . he's dead . . . Boom! That's how you do it!" The latest round of grunts from Mark sounded like some sort of half-assed war charge.

He and Nathan battled endlessly for top score on *World of Warcraft*. This latest fight had gone on for two hours, and whoever lost had to drink whatever liquor remained in a red Solo brand cup that sat between the two of them like a threat. The vodka from Nathan's dad's liquor cabinet turned out to be cookie-dough flavored specialty vodka with a Russian label. It tasted like farts mixed in gasoline. I took one shot and refused to drink any more, but everyone else didn't seem to mind the awful taste.

"So, the party's happening now?" Josh asked. He stretched out face up on the bed, sounding bored.

"Yep."

"How many people did they invite again?"

"Not enough. They didn't invite us." I laughed.

"I kinda wish they had," Josh said.

"They're trolls," I replied.

He chuckled. "Tell me something I don't know. But I do wish they'd stop leaving us out."

A lot of the time, I looked at the calendar on my phone and counted the days until I could leave the twins and our boring town in suburbia behind. Two million people lived in Greater Cincinnati—probably more than that, if you counted the fringes of Dayton, OH. There had to be more to life than a small town where everyone was rich, warm, comfortable, and focused on beating each other for scholarships, grades, state championship football titles, and awards given out by the local newspapers. It all just resembled a boring game—one I didn't want to play anymore.

"You know—" Josh ran his tongue along his front teeth, "—we could show up."

"Show up?"

"And crash the party." He looked over at me. "It's your house. There's nothin' stoppin' us."

Josh liked to drop the "g" from his words when he drank.

I rolled my eyes. "They'll stop us."

"'Nd do what? Kick us out? Call the fuckin' cops? Start some kind of fight?" He also liked to switch up his voice and cuss a lot, so that he sounded tough. Trouble was that Josh wasn't tough. Not really. A long scar decorated his shin from the one time he'd gotten into a fight after school in the second grade, but for most his life, Josh shrank from conflict. He talked big, but he never followed through.

"Yeah. Call the cops. Exactly," I replied.

"I'm not scared." He paused. "Not scared at all. We should go the fuck over there."

"Come on," I said. "You don't mean that."

"What if I do?"

"It's not worth it. No reason to make things worse. They're already horrible enough—"

"Whatever. We should still go over there." Josh rose up and blocked my view of Mark and Nathan, both still shaking and shouting as they started the final push to win the level. With their energy level, this could go on for hours.

"I bet Laine will be there," Josh said.

"She probably will." No need to add the insider knowledge that I had confirming the fact.

"I saw her the other day with Evan out in the parking lot. I don't think they're very happy."

"Why would I care about that?" I took special care with my voice to make sure I sounded disinterested. Then I bit the inside of my cheek and hoped he believed it.

"Because you've had a crush on her since seventh grade."

Fuck. Time to think of a lie. Something. Anything.

"I don't have a crush on her. I don't."

"Oh, so you've all the sudden stopped liking her?"

"Yep." I popped my jaw and kept my eyes on the ceiling. If he couldn't meet my eyes, he wouldn't see the truth. Right?

"Dude, I'm your friend. Your best friend. I see the way you stare at her. You did it again today at lunch."

"I don't stare at her. I don't!" Those last words sounded like a lie, even to me.

"Nice. So. You do care." Josh poked me in the back. "Anyway. Seemed like the argument between Laine and Evan was pretty intense."

"Laine's hot," said Mark, sounding like a zombie. Josh flipped his head in Mark's direction, but Mark didn't turn around. Instead, the game got louder as Mark and Nathan started another shooting sequence.

"She is hot," Josh admitted as he turned back to me. "More than hot. Didn't she book a new modeling job?"

"I don't know," I lied again. "I guess."

"Yep, something with Macy's," Josh said. "Probably got it since she modeled in Paris last summer," Josh said.

"She did not."

"She did. I saw it on Twitter."

"Like Twitter is believable. People say fake shit on Twitter all the time. Like all the times people say some celebrity died, and they didn't."

"Whatever. I have 1500 fuckin' followers." Josh liked to remind people of this statistic. He kept track of it the way some people kept track of stock prices, and he checked his phone every afternoon after class just so he could see his number rise and fall. "How many do you have?"

I sighed. "Twenty. But I never tweet."

"Exactly." He said this as if he'd just made a case-winning argument in court. "Trust me. I saw it there."

"You have 1500 followers because you followed all

those people first, and then they were nice and followed you back. Do you even know who half those people are?"

"What I'm sayin' is that I have a lot of sources. Get information from everywhere."

"Look, not all those people are legit sources."

He dismissed me with a wave. "Doesn't mean they aren't telling the truth."

"Why the fuck are we arguing about your Twitter followers, Josh?"

"You can think whatever you want," Josh replied. "I'm just sayin' I tapped a broad range of people for my information. That's how I know that shit is real."

I shook my head, but didn't try to further correct him. Laine did pick up the occasional modeling job, but only regionally, and the furthest away she'd ever modeled was for a job in Chicago. She booked mostly print, and some small runway for a few designers in town—one of whom had a studio in Milford, and liked to design dresses for beauty queens. Again, I knew all of this just from Facebook stalking, the best and worst thing to ever happen to the Internet. Maybe I would do some more of that over the weekend.

Couldn't hurt. And yes, I was a little bit obsessed. Okay, a lot.

"That's it." Josh stood up from the bed. "We're goin' over there. Now. Right now. No more fuckin' waitn'."

I glanced from him to foot of the bed, where Mark and Nathan continued to battle. Josh followed my eyes, and then poked me in the shoulder.

"Do you really want to stay here and watch them play while all we do is drink?"

"No." I shrugged. "I guess not."

"Good. At least our lives aren't going to be totally stupid this weekend." He grabbed my arm, pulled me up off the bed, and propelled me to the door without another glance at our video gaming friends.

We heard the music before we got to the house. It rocked through the brick, shook the window glass, and sounded like a mix of rap and techno spun by a Hollywood DJ. My stepbrothers must have put the music on full blast with the sound system they got for Christmas. That thing had enormous speakers.

I had to park at the end of the street because a purple truck and silver 1999 Ford Mustang occupied the two parking spots in the driveway, and a thick sea of luxury sixteenth birthday presents, including souped-up trucks, designer SUVs and custom imports lined the rest of Ammunition Ridge.

"Well, we know your brothers are popular," Josh said. "Really popular."

He slammed the passenger door shut and put his gloved hands up to his mouth to cover his face from the cold.

"Stepbrothers," I corrected him.

"Okay. Stepbrothers," he said from behind the glove. "Jesus Christ, it's fuckin' freezin'. It's like, negative ten around here."

The snow crunched under our feet as we walked up the concrete path to the house. When we got within ten feet, Josh hesitated, as if he wanted to go around the back of the house and head in through the patio just off the kitchen. I shook my head.

"We'll go in the front door." I already had my key out, and I popped open the door a second later.

Just like the music, a roar of laughter and conversations I couldn't place filtered through the house to the front door. Josh and I walked through the foyer, past the living room, by the winding open staircase, and into the large kitchen. From there, we only had to open a white door and head down about fifteen steps to find the party.

"How many people do you think are down there?" Josh shoved his gloves in his pocket, took off his jacket, and hung it on a hook near the breakfast nook. He didn't ask if he should, because he knew that he could. In fact, he was the only person at Heritage High who had ever seen my bedroom.

I shrugged, then dropped my own scarf, jacket, and gloves over the back of one the chairs at the breakfast nook table. "Maybe seventy-five."

"Can the basement fit that many people?"

"This is the *basement* we're talking about. It covers this whole house."

We both stood there for a few more minutes, listening. The laughter stayed loud, and the music didn't switch away from rap with a strong bass line. Whoever was downstairs was having a good time. No, a great time. They might even have been having one of the best parties of senior year, and the thought made me cringe.

I always stood on the outskirts of everything while everyone else had a better time than me. The popular guys had it so easy. They got chicks just by blinking. They laughed their way through high school, smoking pot, drinking, and somehow getting away with everything. They acted like nothing bothered them while I struggled to find words to say to a girl.

And now, here I stood, eighteen years' old, and intimidated by a house party. In. My. Own. House. What kind of bullshit was that?

I looked Josh in the eye. "You ready?"

"To what? Just go down there?"

"What? You're scared now? You're the one who insisted we crash this thing."

"Well, yeah, but that was before—" He broke off, and rubbed the back of his neck with his left hand.

"Before what?" My head tilted. All I had to do was keep up a brave act, even though inside I wanted to turn around and drive back to the *World of Warcraft* party. Maybe if I acted like I didn't care, I wouldn't, in the end.

"There are just going to be so many people down there."

"Yeah." My voice dripped with sarcasm. "They invited, like, the whole senior class. Probably the whole school."

Blake and Bruce had a way of doing things in a grand way, a part of their constant quest to ascend to the top of the Heritage High social heap. Judging by the sounds coming from downstairs, their efforts this time might have worked quite well.

I lifted my hand to open the basement door.

"Wait." Now Josh's voice turned high pitched, and some color faded from his face. "What are we going to do once we get down there?"

I thought about it. "Act like they invited us?"

"That won't work."

"Pretend like one of them got an urgent phone call?"

"Come on, Geoff. This has to be good. Really fuckin' good."

"I don't know." I sighed. "You're the one who had this bright idea. You figure it out."

Josh's thin lips twisted back and forth. Then, after a moment, his eyes widened. "Okay. I've got it." He turned and his eyes swept over the kitchen, looking for something. "Where does your dad—I mean, David—keep his liquor? Like, the good liquor."

"In a cabinet in the dining room."

"Why don't we get some and bring it down to the party?"

"He'll notice." I leaned my back up against the island as I considered his idea. "Yeah. David would definitely notice."

"Hmm. We could bring them all pizza."

I shook my head. "No way. We'll just go down there, and act like we're supposed to be there."

"That's going to piss them all off."

I smiled. "Exactly."

"Are you sure we should?"

"What are you talking about? You're the one who had this idea. Now you're going to back out?"

"Well, I mean—"

"Dude, whatever."

With a flourish, I pulled open the door and led Josh down the steps. I got a good look at the basement about halfway down the staircase, and I stopped on the third step from the end. Josh bumped into me as I did. By then, the conversation and laughter from the party had died, and only the deafening beat from a Kanye West song remained. More than fifty people stared at me, smelling like a stew of marijuana, incense, and stale pizza. I saw faces from the senior and junior class, most of them the popular and the beautiful people of Heritage. Open bottles of liquor littered the coffee table in the small living room area to my right, and still more of those bottles lay in a haphazard mess on the bar. Blunts painted a small table that sat just below the dartboard on the far wall. One girl had her shirt off and stood next a group of boys in her bra.

Wild party.

There was no doubting that one. Damn, I wished I'd been invited to this, but once again I'd been left out. The popular kids got everything they wanted, and I hated them even more for it in that moment. Assholes. Squinting at the silent group, I wondered for a second if I might get a contact high from all the pot. Might be kind of nice if I did.

"Don't mind me."

"What the fuck are you doing?' Bruce's voce resonated over Kanye West. He sat in between a couple of junior girls on the leather couch in the far end of the room. One girl had curly black hair, a nose ring, and breasts that threatened to tumble out of her V-neck sweater as she leered at me from the crook of his right arm.

"Geoff Megadeth," Monica said, from inside the crowd of guys gathered near a couple of empty cans of cheap beer on the bar. Laine stood next to her in a pair of dark jeans, but I didn't let myself acknowledge anything about. If I did, I might lose focus on what I wanted to do next.

"That's me," I said in their direction. God, that nickname was so uncreative. You'd think they might come up with something better. Couldn't they get over that, and move on to something else?

"What do you want?" Bruce asked again.

"Well, this is a party, right?" I reached out to a table next to the steps, grabbed a beer, and popped open the can. "I love parties."

"You're not invited."

A few murmurs spun through the crowd. Some people giggled. Others gawked at Josh and me. A few looked uncomfortable and some stepped backward, as if to give the showdown between Bruce and me more space. Everyone knew life inside Heritage High meant being a part of a hierarchy, just like I did. Blake and Bruce enjoyed the comforts of pseudo friendships with people they thought mattered while Josh, Nathan, Mark and I swam along the bottom next to the band geeks, computer freaks and poor kids. A fight between the two circles always made for good entertainment.

"Sure I'm invited," I told Bruce after a few seconds of stalemate. "This is my house."

He stood up from the couch and took a purposeful step toward me. "Get the fuck out of here, Geoff."

"I'm not going to—"

"Get the fuck out of here, now."

"Come on," I said locking my eyes with his as I took I sip of the beer. It tasted like sour water, and I wanted to spit it out, but I didn't. "You don't mean that."

"This isn't a party for you, or assholes like you."

"Come on, Blake," Bruce said, but he shut up when Blake shot him a glare.

"You weren't invited, asswipe." His voice grew louder, until it made Kanye West sound like a whining child. "And if you'll go on ahead and leave—"

My laughter cut him off. He took another step toward me.

"Seriously, you aren't invited. And you know not to come in the basement. What the fuck do you want, Geoff?"

"Oh nothing," I said. "Just wanted to let you know—the neighbor was complaining." I switched my attention to the rest of the crowd. "About the loud music."

Bruce crossed his arms and gave me one of those looks that told me he didn't buy what I was selling. I had to try harder. A lot harder.

"I think they called the cops." I glanced back at Josh, looking for someone to back me up on my lie. He nodded in agreement. "Yeah. They did. Said they could hear the music in their kitchen."

"Which neighbor?"

"The Andersons. Mrs. Anderson." I looked down at my watch. "That was about fifteen minutes ago. I think—well, I wouldn't be surprised if the cops showed up soon. She was really pissed. Like, *really* pissed."

"I didn't think she was home." Bruce sounded skeptical.

"I took the call," I told him, making sure I didn't waver on my lie. "Didn't I, Josh?"

Josh answered my question with an emphatic nod.

Bruce still didn't seem convinced. "You don't—"

"I tried to stop her from calling," I said. "But I don't think she wanted to listen to me."

"Shit," Evan said from the back of the room. "I gotta—I can't get arrested again. I don't want to risk my scholarship."

"I should leave, too," a brunette junior girl who was

sitting on the large leather chair near the sofa, said. "I can't get arrested again—" She stood up and brushed pizza crumbs and marijuana off her skirt. "Oh my God. I really should go."

"Wait." Blake held up his hand from his place by the stereo. He turned the volume down. "We don't know she called. Geoff could just be lying."

"I'm not lying."

Bruce's lips twisted. "I bet you are, you little piss ant."

"Do you really want to find out?" I asked.

"I don't," said the junior girl as she pulled on her puffy red Columbia jacket. "I really don't."

"Yeah, I'm leaving, too," said a girl right beside her. "Where did I put my coat?"

"Where did I put my shirt?" asked the girl in the bra. She began searching the room for it, and I had to bite back a grin. Her boobs looked kind of funny as they bounced around in black lace.

"Goddamn it," Bruce muttered.

Once I heard that, I full on smiled. Nothing could break up a party like the threat of the cops. It was funny, really, how easy it was to do it. They were all lemmings—all followers.

"Nice work," Josh said under his breath.

Chapter four

WEDNESDAY, FEBRUARY 6

THAT WINTER, I would stumble through the aisles of Target three times a week. I couldn't really place why I wound up there so much. Sometimes I just went there and walked around to pass the time. Something about the wide shelves and red paint attracted me. It was a good place to get lost and blow the $50 a week David and my mom gave me for chores around the house. Plus, Target had cheap graphic tees and a decent video game selection. Just so long as I stayed away from the Megadeth t-shirts.

I picked out a shirt that said, "Trust me, I'm a doctor" and walked, as usual, to the video game section. Racks of games stretched out on one side, while rows of computer parts and accessories lined the other. My hand skimmed through the games, but I didn't really see them. Shoppers strolled past me on their way to the toy section and the food, and boredom arrived. Maybe I'd buy this game, or that game. Or none of them at all. I'd been there a few minutes when a twist of my stomach told me to look up.

Laine stood at the end of the row.

"Hey. What are you doing here?" I asked, as I walked over to her. She had one hand on her hip, a red basket in her other hand, and a large grin on her face. And, God, she wore that leather jacket like she'd just come from a Victoria's Secret catalog photo shoot.

She held up the basket, half full of makeup, shoes, and books. "Buying stuff. Since that's what people do here."

"Just like how they study in a library."

"Exactly." She grinned. "Sometimes they study there."

"Other times, they just go there to get away from people."

She stepped closer and everything about her body language enticed me, from the smile that danced on her lips to the way her body showed off her breasts. And again, she smelled like bubblegum lip-gloss. Damn, I was going to have to bottle that scent. "Is that what you do in the library?"

"No," I whispered.

"I thought maybe you liked to be alone."

"Well," I faltered, my voice growing weak as my neck flushed, "I don't know—"

"Like here in Target," she said, her voice low. "Do you like to be alone in Target?"

"Well, I mean…" I struggled to find something to say as I realized her voice had just given me a hard-on.

Shit.

Her eyes widened after another second of uncomfortable stuttering from me. "How's the selection?"

"Of what?"

"Video games. Computer parts."

"Oh, right," I replied. "It's fine. Good. No, great. You know, since it's Wal—I mean, Sam's—I mean, since it's Target."

She giggled, and I wanted to disappear into the floor. I really needed to stop getting so flustered whenever she was around me. I was starting to annoy myself. Not a good look for me—even if she was the most intimidating girl in school. I needed to pull my ass together.

"Hmm." She took a few steps past me, and out of instinct I followed her lead. "I was thinking of getting something myself."

"Like what?"

She paused above the games marked with a 'M'. "*Mass Effect 3*."

I gawked at her. "You do not want to buy that game."

"Why not?"

Her fingers flipped through the cases, and I watched her do it with interest. This must have been a joke. Surely, there couldn't have been something for sale in this section of Target that she'd want. She belonged somewhere else, like trying on cheap boots in the shoe section, or scooping up trendy necklaces in accessories. And didn't she like scarves? Target sold plenty of those.

"I've played all the other ones," she said. "My older brother, Todd, got me into it when he came home from Kent State at Christmas."

"Really?" I didn't even try to hide the surprise in my voice. I had so much trouble believing that the school goddess liked a first-person shooter game about the end of the world. She wouldn't want something like that. She wouldn't even know about a game like that. Right?

"You know," she said as she pulled *Mass Effect 3* off the rack. Her eyes didn't meet mine. "I've told you before. You really should stop being so judgmental of people."

"Why do you think that? I'm not judgmental."

"Yeah, you are." She slipped the game into the basket. "You like to put people in boxes, don't you?"

"No."

"Do people put you in a box?"

"No," I replied. "Well—I mean—kind of . . ."

"I think it's a defense mechanism."

"It is not." We fell into step together as she started walking down the aisle and away from the electronics section of the store.

"You know, not everyone at Heritage is so bad, Geoff."

What the hell did she mean by that?

"I wouldn't say I like putting people in boxes," I said after a few moments of awkward silence. "And I just know my place in the world."

Laine stopped in between a rack of workout clothes and the shoe section, which already showed a display of sandals. She narrowed her eyes at me. "And what place is that?"

"I'm a dork. You're popular. We don't mix."

"Pfft. That is such a stupid rule. This is senior year. We've been at the same school together for years, and it's almost over. What does all that stuff matter?"

"I think it matters to a lot of people still."

"That's where I think you're wrong." She braced herself against the end cap of shoes, and studied me. "By the way, that was an awesome stunt you pulled the other night."

"Stunt?" I feigned ignorance.

"Yeah. Faking the police call."

"It wasn't fake."

She crossed her arms, and grinned. "Did they ever come? Monica said Blake told her they didn't."

"They came," I lied.

"Sure they did. I believe you." A conspiratorial look crossed her face. "I know Mrs. Anderson lives three houses away from yours. There's no way she heard the party. It wasn't that loud." She shrugged. "Not that it matters. It wasn't that great of a party, anyway."

"What? You don't like Blake and Bruce's epic parties?"

She laughed.

"Smelled like it had some good pot," I said.

"I don't smoke pot, Geoff."

"Me either," I admitted, then looked down at my watch. "Oh, wow. It's already like five p.m."

"It is? Really?" She backed away from me, and her eyes darted around the empty aisles, as if she expected to see someone creeping up on us.

"Yep."

"Whoops, I gotta go. Now." She moved into the aisle. I followed her, curious about the drastic change in her voice and mannerisms. Did I hear panic in her voice? Why had her eyes widened so much?

"Laine, wait—"

She shook her head. "I'm gonna be late."

"For what?"

"Dinner," she said quickly. "I'm supposed to have dinner with Evan's family."

"Evan." The word tasted like rotting onions in my mouth. "Yeah, well, I wouldn't want you to be late for that." The panic I heard in her voice reminded me of that day in the hallway, and the bruise. "What about your arm? Is it any better?"

"My arm?" Now she really sounded panicked. "Why are you asking about that?"

"I don't know. I just saw the bruise the other day, and it's been bothering me. Is it still there?" It was one of the many times in life I wished I had laser vision, or the ability to read minds.

"Oh, that. Totally healed. See ya later, Geoff," she said, already ten feet away from me. She turned, and kept walking to the front of the store. I watched her round ass get smaller and smaller as she took the smell of bubblegum and floral perfume with her.

Once again, I was all alone.

THURSDAY, FEBRUARY 14

OF ALL THE days I hated at Heritage, Valentine's Day was one I hated the most. Every day of the week leading up to it, sophomore members of the Student Council sat in the front lobby selling candy grams and carnations at a large table decorated with a big sign. They sold these with gusto, as if they relished this job the same way a baker relished a new recipe. No one escaped the sales pitch.

"Would you like to buy a candy gram?" a girl with long black curls shouted at everyone who walked by between 7:45 a.m. and the first bell at 8:15 a.m. "How about a carnation?"

"They're only three dollars," a guy with braces and a blue polo shirt chimed in, a plastic smile affixed to his face. "Goes to a great cause."

They never added that not getting one of these during first period on Valentine's Day equaled being branded a loser. Oh no, they never mentioned that.

Each sale acted as a fundraiser for the Student Council Scholarship, a $500 award given each year to a senior. Most years, the valedictorian won the money, which meant Harvard-bound Nichole Reese would get it this year. Damn her. She had a better GPA than me by two tenths of a point, cried when she didn't make an A on a test, and held the state record in tennis. We were not friends. Not even frienemies.

We competed in an open war.

I'd heard people talk about Valentine's Day in almost every conversation for the two days prior to the fourteenth. It had covered the halls like slime, and strangled the conversation between classes.

"Do you think Greg will send me a carnation?"

"I'm not sure who to send my candy grams to this year."

"Oh my God, I just, well, I was thinking I might tell Kevin how I feel about him on Valentine's Day."

"I can't believe Amanda broke up with me right before Valentine's. She's such a bitch."

"I hate this day. Don't even want to think about it. Maybe I'll tell my parents I'm sick, and stay home eating chocolate."

Which is why today, Valentine's Day itself, my stomach constricted as I sat in AP English. All around me, classmates sat patient, expectant, and awaiting their deliveries. I heard Heather Smith tell Kendall Ace she thought she might get a candy gram from Bruce this year. Kendall then confided her hopes for one from Vince Stephens. Other students speculated on who would get candy grams and carnations, the same way people talked about who might win the NCAA. Even Nichole Reese, who sat diagonal to me, seemed excited this year, a wide smile on her face. Disgusted and annoyed, I shook my head, opened up my binder, and waited for Mr. Langston to start his lesson on British poetry.

"Good morning, class." Langston stood up from his desk. He wore a cheesy but festive red sweater with white trim around the collar and cuffs. He had minimal crumbs on his chest, and part of me was proud of him for that. "Please turn to page 175 in your text. The first paragraph." A whoosh flooded the room as we all followed his orders. "Nichole, can you please read?"

"Yes, Mr. Langston." Nichole Reese sucked in a large breath. "Classical British poetry can first be traced . . ."

She read several paragraphs from the text about the definition of classical poetry in great detail, before three sharp raps at the door rescued us. A collective rumble passed through the class, and a couple of kids giggled. We all knew what the knocks meant.

"Well, I guess Cupid is here," Mr. Langston said as he walked over to the door. He said this in a cheesy way, like it should come as a surprise. When he opened the door, a boy and girl from Student Council stood on the other side, one holding multicolored carnations and the other holding a basket full of small chocolate baskets.

"Candy grams and carnations!" they shouted in

unison. I saw a few girls' faces turn pink with anticipation.

"Well, feel free to deliver them," said Mr. Langston as he moved out of the way of the door. "I won't stand in the way of true love."

I had to stop myself from rolling my eyes because Mr. Langston said "true" like "twue" and "love" like "wuv." Just hearing it grated my ears. Why did he always have to speak to us the same way he would talk to five-year-olds? He always added a condescending flair to everything. Thank God I'd read a chapter ahead in the text, and school came easy to me. I couldn't have stood his insipid teaching any other way.

"Here's one for Heather," the girl holding carnations said. Heather got up from her desk and took the carnation, just like an actress would take her award at the Golden Globes—even sinking into a long bow once she had the flower in hand.

"I have chocolates for Josh," the boy said.

"Ooooohhhhhhhhh!" tittered a few of the other kids in the class.

When I glanced back at Josh, his face had turned redder than Mr. Langston's sweater. Sheepish, he slid out of his fifth row seat and retrieved the box of Whitman's candy. I shot him a grin, and knew I'd tease him about it later.

"This one is for Kendall."

"And look, one for Adam."

And so it went, for another five minutes. Students waited to hear their names, and then bounded to the front to accept their gifts. I tuned most of it out by doodling on the back page of a worksheet in my binder, and it almost worked.

Until I heard my own name.

"I have some candy for Geoff Miller."

My head snapped up, and I stared at the front of the room. "What?"

"Yeah, Geoff," the girl said. "The last candy gram in the basket is for you."

"What?" Several students in the class laughed. People didn't give me things on Valentine's Day. Especially not things they bought from the Student Council. "What?"

"Just go up there and get it, Geoff," Mr. Langston said, with a sweep of his fat arm.

"Geoff Megadeth," I heard a student whisper a few rows behind me.

I got out of my seat, walked to the front, and retrieved the small gold box, large enough to hold four chocolates. A fancy red bow tied a small white note to the box. I read it under my desk when I got back to my seat.

Happy Valentine's Day, Mr. Judgmental.

I found her in the parking lot across the street from campus after school, just about to get in her RAV4. She stood out from the rest of the crowd in a bright blue puffy coat. For some reason, the coat made her hair remind me of a sunflower.

Once she'd finished talking to her friends I walked right up to her, faking my confidence, and hoping she wouldn't notice that I'd rehearsed my introduction to her about one hundred times in my head before I'd say it aloud.

"So. Mr. Judgmental."

She whirled around, a smile already on her face, and

leaned against the open car door.

"That your new nickname for me, Laine?"

"Depends."

"Thanks for the chocolate."

She shrugged. "Best chocolates three bucks can buy."

"I'd like to add that I stretched them out. Made them last for eight bites, instead of four." Of course, I left out the part about how I tucked the note into my back jeans pocket and planned to save it in the bottom of my sock drawer. I could be a sentimental schmuck like that sometimes.

"I'm sure that was torture," she deadpanned. "How ever did you manage?"

"Did you get enough carnations to make a bouquet this year?" I cursed myself as soon as I said it. Goddamn it, I knew way too much about her. *Way* too much. And, worst of all, here I was letting her know it. I had to stop that shit.

"You remember that?" She tossed me a quizzical expression.

"Well . . . yeah . . . I mean . . ." I struggled to come up with an excuse that didn't end in me admitting how much I'd stalked her on Facebook. I had to think of some excuse. Any excuse. I just had to get out of creepy territory, and fast. "I just remember something . . . someone said something about it."

"Yeah, well, I was so stupid sophomore year," she admitted. "I kinda strung a bunch of guys along."

"I'm sure they didn't mind."

"You'd be surprised." Her hands tapped out a beat on the car door seal. Around us, the parking lot had almost emptied. Seventy-five juniors and seniors parked there every day, but right then, only about ten were left. I liked that. Less of a chance I'd have to give some gossipy kid a reason for why I stood there, talking to the most captivating girl in a ten-mile radius.

"Listen," she said after a couple of beats. "I need to get home and get ready to cheer at the basketball game, so can we talk more later? Maybe on Facebook?" She winked at me, and my mouth went dry from panic.

Oh shit. Had she figured out the reason why I knew so much about her?

"Facebook?" I feigned innocence.

"Yeah. Facebook. Aren't we friends on there?"

We weren't. I knew it. Most of my Facebook stalking of this girl happened via third party comments and photo tags. A couple of times, I'd hovered the mouse over the friend request button, but I always backed out before I went through with it. Better to be outside her loop of friends than wind up in Facebook purgatory—a forever pending friend request with no answer from her.

"I don't know."

"I'll friend request you," she said as she put one leg in the car. "Are you on Twitter?"

"Yep."

"Me too. Instagram?"

"Who isn't?"

"Perfect." She sat down in the driver's seat. "I'll talk to you later, Geoff."

"Bye."

She closed the door, started the engine, waved, and pulled out of the parking lot. About an hour later, my phone buzzed.

She'd followed through with her promise.

Chapter five

WEDNESDAY, FEBRUARY 20TH

"AH, MR. MILLER. PLEASE sit down." Mr. Henderson looked up from his desktop computer and flashed a yellow-toothed smile at me. I shut the door and sat down in a metal chair with too much stuffing in the bottom cushion.

"I got a note that you wanted to see me," I replied. My words came out as more of a question than a statement.

"Yes. Well. We're meeting with all the seniors individually." Mr. Henderson folded his hands on the desk, and gave me a slight grin. "Mrs. Lawrence is meeting with the girls, and I'm meeting with the boys. And I'll meet with you again before the year's up, since you are one of the top students here at Heritage."

"Again?"

"Yes, Geoff. More than once. We meet with the top five students more than once."

I gave him a plastic smile. Repeated meetings with

the school guidance counselor? Another perk of my status as class salutatorian, and just what I wanted.

"I see you are going with UVA," Mr. Henderson said as he opened the thick manila folder that must have contained every aspect of my twelve years of life in the Heritage school system. "Charlottesville. Lovely place in the fall."

"Guess I am going to find out."

He blinked at me, three times. "Of course, we are very proud of you and your accomplishments."

"Thanks."

"Heritage is an excellent school system. We really have given you a rigorous education." He looked down at the chart. "And, I see here, you are in all advanced classes."

"Not just advanced classes. I'm taking mostly AP classes this year." I paused. "Doesn't it say that in my file?"

"Right. Of course it does." He closed the folder.

I glanced at the clock. How long was this meeting going to last? Too bad I couldn't think of any old excuse to get myself out of a meeting with the guidance counselor. They called bullshit on students faster than the rest of the teachers.

"I'm a little worried about your grades this year, Mr. Miller."

My eyes snapped back in his direction. "Why?"

"Your teachers tell me you're listless. Bored. And your grades are—"

"I have straight As."

"There are As, Mr. Miller, and there are As. You have the former."

"Huh?"

He drummed his fingers on the desk. "Some of your teachers have said your overall percentages in their classes have slipped. For example, Mr. Langston told me that you had an overall 98 percent in English at the beginning of the year. Now, you have a 95."

Not Mr. Langston again.

"A 95 is still an A," I pointed out.

"But it's not the A you used to have." His voice turned warmer, more fatherly. "It's not what we're used to from you." He leaned across the desk. "I want to help you figure out what is bothering you. Why you're slipping this year."

I frowned, and sat back further in my chair. "But I'm not slipping."

"Have you given any real thought as to what you want to major in next year at Virginia?"

"Umm . . ."

Mr. Henderson squinted at me. "Well, you must have some sort of an idea of what you want to do with your life."

"A little." Sinking further into the chair, I rubbed my eyebrow. "I've thought about it some."

"And what are you interested in the most?"

Jesus. Each question that came out of his mouth sounded loaded, as if at any moment he wanted to make me fall over a verbal land mine. "I like history. Russian History. Communism. World War Two." I thought about it some more. "Maybe I'll try to do something with that."

"Something with Russian History?"

"Maybe. But I also like writing."

"You're good at Math, Mr. Miller."

I licked my lips. "Yeah, Math is okay, I guess."

"You're in, what—AP Calculus and AP Bio this year?"

Oh. So he had read my transcript. Imagine that. "Yeah, Mr. Henderson, I am."

"Seems like a kid like you should major in Engineering or Bio Chemistry. Maybe work for P&G when you grow up." His voice sounded firm and final, as if he'd come to the answer of my future through one quick calculation in his head.

"Everyone around here works for P&G," I pointed out. It wasn't too much of a stretch from the truth. Most of my classmates lived in nice houses and went to summer camps on money made by their corporate-ladder ascending parents. P&G held the purse strings for most of Greater Cincinnati.

"It's a perfectly good company," he said, tapping his fingers on the desk. "Excellent company. Fortune 500. And that's saying something."

"I know, but—"

"You should be happy to work for a company like that one." He tapped his fingers on the folder that held my life inside. "You know, seems to me like a waste of a perfectly good education if you go to Virginia and major in something other than Law, Business, Science or Engineering. Those kinds of degrees get a person somewhere in life."

"Like a job here?"

Mr. Henderson narrowed his eyes. "Are you being funny with me, Mr. Miller?"

"No." I shook my head. "I just don't want to be stuck here in Cincinnati for the rest of my life." I wrinkled my nose at the thought. "Yuck."

"Most people wouldn't call life here 'being stuck.'"

"I would."

"It sounds to me like you are being a little judgmental about the opportunities you have out there. Life isn't about that." He cleared his throat. "You'll get a lot further if you stop and think about others. Stop, get to know them, and realize you aren't better than anyone else."

"I don't think I am better than anyone else," I insisted.

"What are you going to do with a degree in Russian History?" He blanched. "The Cold War's over."

"I know, but I think—"

"Virginia is an expensive school." He glanced at the ceiling, as if doing another math problem in his head. "It could cost your parents about a hundred thousand dollars when you are finished."

"But I got some scholarships." I gulped. Just the week before, I'd shuddered when I'd seen the packet breakdown the school sent me of expected expenses for the 2014 freshman class. Books alone could cost $700 bucks—used. "I know. It's not cheap."

"The point is, if you're going to spend money like that it is important to think about what value you're getting. Just getting a degree in history won't pay the bills, Mr. Miller. You have to have a plan, and execute it. That's the best way to get things done."

"You don't know that."

He laughed. "Oh, I most certainly do. I've been in the adult world longer than you. I know a thing or two about how things work."

"So what are you saying?"

"If you are confused about your major, I suggest you reconsider Virginia. Why spend all that money?" He leaned forward, his beady eyes locked on mine. "Have you thought about Gateway Technical College?"

"Technical college?" I almost spat out the words.

He sized me up again. "What? Think you're too good for technical college? What did I just say about thinking you're better than anyone else?"

"Well, but I am better," I struggled with my answer. "Um. Yeah. I'm salutatorian."

"Right." He cleared his throat. "Number two. Not number one."

"But I mean, I got into Virginia," I replied, aghast. "Virginia! Doesn't that mean something to you?"

"It shows me you know how to write a good essay. And perform well on a standardized test."

"Wasn't this conversation supposed to . . . suppose to help me?"

"It's not helping you, Mr. Miller?"

Why was he always calling me Mr. Miller? God, it was as bad as "Geoff Megadeth." Couldn't these people be more creative? "Well, I don't think it is. I'm not trying to limit myself at all. I'm trying to get away from Robert Hill, and Cincinnati. For good."

"Technical colleges are a good place to go for someone who can't decide on their future, and who doesn't have a plan, Mr. Miller. When you get out in the real world, you'll discover that it's not where you went, but what you know, and how you use it. Not just book knowledge. Practical knowledge." He waved a dismissive hand. "Just tell me you'll consider it."

I sucked in a deep breath, and leaned in closer to his

desk. "Okay," I lied. "I'll consider it."

"And you mean that?"

"Yes," I lied again. "I'll consider it. You're right. Why limit myself?"

A satisfied look came over his face. "That's what I like to hear, Mr. Miller, that's what I like to hear." He nodded at the door. "You can go back to class now."

SATURDAY, FEBRUARY 23

A TEXT FROM Josh broke up the monotony of polishing the silver, a chore I did every Saturday. David and my mom had so much of it, with an antique silver service for six, multiple trays, and a silver spoon collection. Between the silver, mopping the tiled floors, cleaning the bathrooms, mowing the lawn in the summer, shoveling snow in the winter, and washing the large windows in the mansion, I made $200 a month. Blake and Bruce were also required to do that kind of work, but they always wanted to get out of it, and often paid me huge chunks of their allowance so they had more free time.

David had told my mother that these chores would be good for me. "It'll teach him some structure. Help him, since he's grown up without a father for so long." I'd overheard them in the living room not long after the wedding. "He needs this. This is what I do with my boys, how I raise them, too. We're all required to help out around here. Trust me."

To my dismay, my mother had agreed. At least it paid well.

2:30PM
Josh: *Dude are you going out tonight?*
Me: *IDK*
Josh: *I asked Allison out. She said she'd meet us at the Levee for a movie.*
Me: *You asked Allison out??*
Josh: *Yeah. Don't bug me about it.*
Me: *Wow. Good call on that*
Josh: *Ugh. U coming to the movie or not?*
Me: *Which movie?*
Josh: *Beautiful Creatures*
Me: *Doesn't look good.*
Josh: *Come on, help me out. It's Allison. Invited Nathan and Mark, too. Group thing.*

I laughed. Ever since Allison surprised Josh with that box of chocolates on Valentine's Day, he'd struggled with asking her out. He kept trying out options on us at lunch, desperate to sound cool and noncommittal all at once. All three of us just told him to man up and ask her out.

Looked like he'd finally taken our advice.

Me: *Fine. What time?*
Josh: *7:30. Movie starts at 8.*
Me: *Meet u there?*
Josh: *Yep*

I put the phone down and turned back to the array of spoons in front of me. David had inherited so many of them from his grandmother, who he'd said traveled the world in her fifties and sixties, and collected the spoons because they didn't take up much space in her luggage. He had ones from China, Holland, England and Canada. Some had pearls, and rhinestones, and other decor. A few looked ancient. I liked to make up stories about where they came from as I polished each one. It helped to break up the tedium, but not the resentment.

"Stop shifting your weight. Just stop. She'll think something is off," I told Josh, who looked like he might vomit at any second as we waited outside the movie theater credit card kiosk later that night.

"Yeah, you look weird," Mark added, the only other person in our group. Nathan canceled about two hours before, saying he had the stomach flu.

"Well, I am kinda nervous," Josh replied. He'd dressed for this "date" in a pair of dark jeans and a gray sweater with a half-zip, but before he picked it out he'd sent me about six Snapchat photos with different outfits, something he'd never ever done before. For once, his shoes had no trace of mud on them. He'd even slicked his hair back, and covered himself in some kind of strong smelling cologne.

"Don't blame you. Allison makes *me* nervous," Mark muttered.

I laughed. Allison Nichols made a lot people nervous. Whippet thin and petite, she dressed in thrift store chic and liked to stare at people with eyes layered in black kohl. One time, I'd caught her walking through the hallway, pulling down student council election posters and putting them in the trash. When I asked her about it, she glared at me, and hadn't given me an answer.

"One time I saw her eating raw eggs for lunch in the cafeteria," Mark said.

"Really?" I said with a skeptical look. I'd heard plenty of gossip over the years about Allison, but that sounded extreme, even for her. "That's not healthy."

Mark held up his hands. "True story. I saw it last year, with my own eyes."

"Scary."

"Shut up, Geoff," Josh said, throwing me a glare. "You too, Mark. She just acts like that so people will leave her the fuck alone. She likes that people make up stuff about her. And you know how people at Heritage are."

Oh, I knew. We all knew.

"I see how it is," I replied. "Now that she likes you, you defend her."

"Yeah, that's how it is."

Mark popped his chin. "Here she comes."

We all turned to face her as she walked up the parking garage steps to the lobby of The Levee. She wore a scowl on her face, black boots, red jeans, and a long gray sweater as she walked through the wide complex rimmed with restaurants, bars, and boutiques that never seemed to stay open for longer than six months. Allison looked pissed and satisfied all at once, and a long pink streak running through the hair on top of her head topped off the look. I wondered how that would go over with the teachers on Monday morning.

"Thanks for inviting me," she said to Josh once she reached him. She smelled like incense. "Really wanted to see this movie."

"Um, yeah," he struggled. "I really wanted to see this,

too."

Liar.

"I've read all the books," she said to all of us. "They're really good. Sooooooo awesome."

"Went on ahead and bought your ticket this afternoon online," Josh said, handing her a small slip. He sounded proud to be able to do this for her.

And that's when I saw the opportunity. "Speaking of books, I need to check out something at Barnes and Noble." I gestured my thumb at the store, like this was an important mission. "Yeah. I need to do that, like, right now."

"I should probably go with him," Mark added.

"What?" Josh frowned at me. "But you can't—"

"Barnes and Noble. Yep, I heard you say something about that earlier."

"It's about my debit card," I said, fumbling to come up with some kind of reasonable excuse. It sounded lame, but whatever. I went with it anyway. "Yeah. I should check this out right away."

"Really?" Now Josh sounded pissed.

"Yeah, I don't want to get into trouble with David and Mom."

"Me too," Mark said. "I should go with him. You know, for moral support."

"I'm sorry I can't make the movie," I said. "You guys have fun."

"Okay . . ."Allison trailed off, a suspicious look on her face.

"I hate you guys," Josh said, clearly nervous and embarrassed.

"No you don't," I replied taking one quick step backward, and then another. "Have fun at the movie." Mark followed me when I gestured to him.

"Are we going to meet up with them after?" Mark asked as I pushed opened the wide doors of the Levee building and walked into the courtyard that led to Barnes and Noble.

"Probably not," I replied. "I mean, isn't this their date, or whatever?"

"I guess it's a date. He likes her a lot." Mark stopped and frowned, deep in thought. "You didn't have any problems with your debit card at Barnes and Noble, right?"

I frowned, and shook my head. "No way. I know that was stupid, but I just said that because I wanted to give them some excuse to be alone."

"Never thought he'd have a crush on Allison Nichols."

I shrugged. "Well, she is kinda hot, if you like that artsy type." I nodded in the direction of the two-story bookstore. "I still want to go there and check it out."

"Yeah, okay," Mark said, and we walked toward the store again. "I wanted to look for a couple of new books."

I chuckled. "What the hell else are we going to do on a Friday night in Cincinnati?"

"I know. God, I wish I was twenty-one. Life doesn't start until you're twenty-one."

"Three more years," I replied, as I flung open the door of the store. "Three more years and we'll dominate this town."

I liked to read. A lot. History. Politics. The modern

classics. F. Scott Fitzgerald. John Grisham. I had a rewards card at Barnes and Noble, and for me, going there was like going to a buffet for a really fat person. I gorged myself on books. Plus, that store was always quiet, so I liked to go there and just think.

These days, I had a lot to think about. What did I really want do with my life? What did I want to major in? Who did I want to be? And what the fuck was going on with me?

I walked straight to the escalator, destined for the political science section. Mark separated from me with a small wave before he disappeared into the music section. I didn't know if I'd see him later or not. Maybe I didn't really care, anyway. I decided not to stress over it, and stopped in front of a long row of books about Republicans vs. Democrats. Books on either side called out the other—shouting, angry titles that always attracted me. I liked books with crazy covers, too

I selected a couple of new books, sat down in an overstuffed chair in the corner, and pulled my phone out of my pocket. I didn't make it through a reading of the first chapter before I decided to check it. Well, "check it" meant I decided to check Facebook. And "checking Facebook" really meant checking Laine Phillip's page.

I did that about six times a day.

This wasn't really my fault, though. She made it all so tempting. Once Laine friended me on her social networks, I might as well have turned into a crack addict who knew a cheap place to get smack. I stalked her page at least twice a day, and most days, even more than that. One night, I skimmed through all the photo albums on her page. Another night, I memorized all the likes and interests. I noticed every new photo she posted on Instagram. My mind cataloged every Twitter reply. Each Facebook check-in acted like a window to her world. All of it went into a big file in my head with her name on it.

My finger unlocked the phone and found the Facebook app. Once it popped up, I scrolled through the usual news feed drivel of mindless statues, photos, complaints and check-ins. When I didn't see her name, I typed it into the search feature. She updated her status 2.5 times a day on average—yes, I did that math in my head. She must have something new to say.

I sucked in a long, winded breath when my eyes saw that she had. She had a new check-in. At the Starbucks. In this Barnes and Noble. "Best peppermint hot chocolate in the world," the status said.

Oh, holy shit.

What were the odds of this kind of luck?

From my place in the comfortable chair, I couldn't see the open-air Starbucks that overlooked the Ohio River, but that didn't matter at all. The air changed all around me, as if electricity now pulsed through it. My heartbeat sped up, then threatened to drop to my knees. Even the way things smelled suddenly seemed different to me—almost metallic—as thoughts raced through my mind.

Should I go talk to her? Did she have friends with her? Would she want company? What if Evan was with her? Did she like to read? Why did she pick a hot chocolate over a café mocha, or a cappuccino? Did she use non-fat milk? Did she like whipped cream?

I had to find it all out. I had to know, and I couldn't let this chance pass. No way. There was only one thing I could do—one thing I had to do. And I could do it.

Right?

Channeling all my energy, I forced myself out of the chair and took a slow walk over to the coffee bar. A few customers lounged in seats near the wall-to-ceiling windows, and four people chatted around a table covered in designer coffee drinks and expensive chocolate desserts. Typical night. I disregarded them and kept my focus on the vision of tumbling blonde hair in front of me.

There, at a center table, Laine sat in front of a venti-sized drink, reading a paperback. She didn't notice me until I stood right next to her, like some sort of a creepy stalker. Well, maybe I was one.

But, whatever.

"Hey, Laine."

She jumped, and closed the book. "Oh, hey. How are you, Geoff?"

"Good." I smiled at her. "I was just walking through the store, and I . . . er . . . well . . . I saw you reading over here, and I thought maybe I'd say hi," I lied. "So. Hi."

"Hi again." She motioned to the empty seat in front of her. "So . . . um . . . do you want to sit down?"

"Sure." I grabbed the back of the seat and sat down as fast as I could, so she wouldn't change her mind. "So, what are you reading?" I asked, even though I could easily read the title from where I stood. I just wanted some way to start this conversation. At any price.

Laine grinned, and tapped her fingers on the book's cover. "*The White Queen*," she said. "One of those history novels about The War of the Roses."

"The War of the Roses?"

"Yep." She closed the book and folded her hands on top of it. "That's the one."

"You really like that stuff, don't you?"

"Well, yeah. I mean, it's pretty great. Lots of drama." She nodded at me. "So, what about you? I mean, what brought you here on a Saturday night?"

"Nothing much." I shrugged, hoping I sounded and looked nonchalant. "Just that some friends wanted to watch a movie, and I didn't care about it, so I came here."

"Do you come here a lot?"

"Enough."

"Sometimes it's nice to be alone," she said, and then took a sip of her coffee. "And I know how you like that."

"Um. Do you like being alone?" My eyes floated to her mouth. God, she had one killer mouth. Even better were the words that came out of it.

"Yeah. Of course I do." She laughed. "Gives me a chance to think. It's calming."

"Yeah it is." I nodded, surprised by her once again. I thought I knew everything about her—what she looked like, her friends, the things she liked to do, and yet every time she opened her mouth, she said something at total odds with what I expected.

"I was looking at books about politics," I said after a moment, just talking to fill up the space. "But there was nothing—nothing worth buying, really." Then I shrugged again. "I don't know. I guess I'm distracted. Just thinking a lot."

"About what?"

"Well," I shrugged again. What the heck? Would it hurt to tell her about at least one of the things bothering me? "I had this weird meeting earlier this week with Mr. Henderson."

She rolled her makeup-heavy eyes. "Yeah. I think

he's making the rounds with the senior guys."

"Have you had your meeting yet with Mrs. Lawrence?"

"No." She snickered. "You mean Crazy Eyes?"

A slow smile spread across my face. "Crazy Eyes?"

Laine closed her eyes, and laughed louder. "I can't . . . I can't really look at her. Her pupils freak me out."

"I know. It's like you can see the whole thing." I shuddered. "It shouldn't be that way. At all."

"Anyway." She gestured to me with her hand, and then sipped her drink some more. "Tell me about this meeting."

"Okay." I leaned in closer. "So, Mr. Henderson calls me in for this meeting, sits me down, and starts asking me all these questions about what I want to do with my life."

"Ugh, that's what Mrs. Lawrence did with Jillian last week."

I grew bolder with my story. "Basically, he wants to know what I'm going to major in, and what I want. So, would you believe that he tells me I should go to Gateway Tech instead of going to UVA and 'wasting my time,' and that I should major in some science class?" I shook my head, and rolled my eyes. "Like, what the fuck is that about?"

"You're salutatorian."

"Well, I am right now." I glanced around at the rest of the people in the coffee shop, as if I were afraid they would snatch it away from me.

"There's no way you shouldn't go to Virginia."

"Thanks for the vote of confidence," I said. "I'm glad to know at least one person believes in me." As I spoke, my eyes drifted to her mouth again. She had such full, pouty lips, and I envied Evan so much because he got to kiss them whenever he wanted. I'd probably never get my chance.

"Ugh, they are so stupid. Those counselors don't know anything." She paused. "We don't have to have all the answers right now. It's not like we have to write it down in blood."

"So," I said, then leaned back in my chair and crossed my arms over my chest, "what are you majoring in next year?"

"Fashion merchandising," she said simply and evenly, as if she'd expected this very question from me. "That's what I've decided."

"Fashion merchandising?" I almost choked on the words.

"Yep." She grinned. "I want to be a fashion designer."

"Does Xavier have a good program for that?"

Shea laughed. "Even if it doesn't, I can always change my mind. It's college. That's what college is about."

Chapter Six

TUESDAY, FEBRUARY 26TH

I CAME HOME from an afternoon playing video games at Nathan's house to an interesting scene.

Blake and Bruce sat at the kitchen table, sulking, with their textbooks open in front of them. David sat at the head of the table, his hands rested on his belly as he looked down his long crooked nose at his two sons. Everything about his body language said "not happy."

"Ah, Geoff." David gave me a rare smile when I darkened the door from the garage to the kitchen. "You're finally home."

"*Finally* home?"

I stopped walking, and leaned against the doorframe. Something inside me warned against stepping any further into the kitchen. Afternoon sunlight might be streaming in through the windows, but an invisible, threatening cloud hung over the table. Even worse, Mom wasn't home. She must have still been at her indoor tennis lesson. Or at the manicurist. She had standing weekly appointments on Tuesdays at both.

"Yes. We've been waiting for you." He rapped his fingers on the table. "Boys, say hello to your stepbrother. Now."

"Hey Geoff," they said in unison. Bruce even added a big plastic smile. They could be charming when they wanted something, and compliant when they were afraid. I wondered which way they felt right then. They didn't turn back to their homework. Nope, they just stared at me like something else only they knew about hung around the room. That bothered me a lot.

And why the fuck was David home, anyway?

"You're home early," I said to David.

"Yes, well." He cleared his throat. "I got a call from the school today." He eyed his trollish sons. "The folks up at Heritage have some concerns about the boys and their grades."

I sucked in a deep breath as my stomach constricted. Living in David's house made me so uneasy. It was like being in a prison yard, and knowing to stay away from the warden. Ever since he'd married my mother we'd danced around each other, both pretending our lives didn't intersect through the breathing of one woman. I guess I was too much of a symbol of her former life, a simpler one in a small house with a rickety metal fence, a patch of garden, an apple tree, and a love that died too early.

"Geoff, did you receive your progress report last week?" David's voice snapped me out of my reverie.

"Of course I did."

Mom had signed it without looking, just as she always did. She knew she didn't have to look, because every quarter I had straight As by my name. Over time, perfect grades had become such an expectation from me that Mom had stopped congratulating me on receiving them. Instead, she signed the quarterly report the same way she signed the check each month for the electric bill. Stupid consistency. Sometimes I thought of faking the grades just to see what she'd say if I came home with a sheet full of Cs and Ds.

"All As, I'm sure," David replied. "We know what to expect when it comes to you. You don't even have to study."

"I wouldn't go that far, but thank you," I said, as I let my backpack drop onto the tiled floor. Even though David had just given me a compliment, I knew I couldn't afford to take it that way. David never said or did anything without an ulterior motive.

"Nonsense, Geoff. You're smart." He rapped his knuckles on the table, as if he wanted to make sure everyone paid attention to what he said next. "Looks like my boys here, however, have fallen very far from the tree this year. Blake? Bruce? What is the GPA I told you I would tolerate for high school?"

"A 2.75," Bruce replied, and as he did, I realized this was the first time I'd seen him so meek. His voice quavered with fear. "You said you wanted to see us each pull at least a 2.75 for senior year."

"That's right. A 2.75. C average." David scooted his chair back from the table, as if he was finished with them. "Shouldn't be hard for two boys in average classes." Then he spoke above their heads, and directed his attention to me. "But today, I get a phone call at work. Pulled me out of a board meeting, if you can believe that. It's the Heritage school secretary. And she tells me Bruce here is carrying a 1.8 right now for his average this year. And Blake is at a 2.10."

David stood up, and walked closer to me. His sons stared at him. "Of course, that is unacceptable—even if their overall GPAs are better. We've already given up the idea of a regular college for these too. They're not going to be a Cavalier, like you. No elite colleges in their futures. Technical school. That's what works for them."

"Okay." All of a sudden, I knew where he wanted this conversation to go. "So. Do you want me to tutor them, or something?"

"Yes, Geoff. You are very smart."

When David stopped a few feet in front of me, his large body and potbelly made me feel claustrophobic in the small alcove between the kitchen and the garage. For a second I wanted to turn around, hop back into my car, and drive away. Not another chore. Not another task. And, ugh, I didn't relish the idea of spending more time with the twins from hell. Still, I stayed. Something about the intensity of his face paralyzed me.

"I'd like you to spend about five hours a week with them," David said. "They need the most help in English, History, and Government. I know you excel in those subjects."

"Yeah, I'm pretty good at them."

"Pretty good?"

I gave him a half-smile. It was the only way I could think of to reply.

"Boys," David called over his shoulder, "if Geoff is your tutor that means you must listen to him. He's going to help you. But I want no complaints, and no teasing. Do you hear me?"

Wait a second. I hadn't agreed to this yet.

"I'll do it, David," I said, desperate to make him aware that this concept still sat in the negotiation stage. "I'll do it, but it is going to take time away from my own studies. And you know, studying for these AP classes takes up a lot of my time."

"I'm sure someone as smart as you can manage."

I kept my face impassive, and tried another tactic. "You know, if you were to hire a tutor for them, someone professional, that would cost a lot of money. A couple hundred a week, I am sure."

A devious smile spread across his lips. Once David squinted his eyes, I knew he'd considered this, and then decided he'd see if I was too stupid to know when I was being taken. "Yes, Geoff, that's right, but you know, I am eager to keep something like this in the family. You know Blake and Bruce better than any tutor I could hire."

"Sounds like it's going to be a job to me."

David regarded me for a few seconds. "Okay. Fine. Let's talk payment." He paused. "How about 25 bucks a week, on top of the money for your chores around the house?"

"No way," I said. "Not enough. This is going to take some work. Who's to say they'll want me to work with them?"

"Oh trust me, Geoff, they'll work with you. They know what this means, and I have their assurances they are going to take the rest of the school year seriously." He turned his head over his shoulder. "Right, boys?"

"Right," they mumbled.

"Two hundred," I said. I had a number in my head we

needed to get to for me to agree.

"How about fifty?"

"One hundred and seventy-five."

"Eighty."

I shook my head. "No. Not enough." I shrugged my shoulders. "You can hire another tutor."

"One hundred and twenty-five."

"One hundred and fifty."

"One hundred and thirty-five a week," David said. "That's my best and final offer, Geoff."

I considered this. Not bad. Enough to go out. Enough to save. Enough. More than enough.

"Okay," I said after a moment. "I'll do it."

David reached out his hand, and I shook it. "Done."

I looked past him to my two stepbrothers, who now regarded me with even more annoyance.

"Great," Blake muttered. "Another chance for Mr. Perfect here to rub his brains in our faces."

A few hours later, my mom found me in my room in front of the computer. "David said you're going to help out the twins."

"Well, he's paying me to do it." I didn't look up from the dreaded outline on the Word document in front of me. The words twisted and turned in front of me, a mess I needed to finish so I could hand it in to Mr. Langston the next day.

She sighed and the wood of the doorframe creaked when she leaned up against it. "You know, honey, David doesn't hate you. Not really."

"Don't remind me."

"I know you are still upset that I married him. I know it was quick. And I know he's hard on you, a lot. But he also respects you, more than he does Blake and Bruce."

"He'll never be anything like my dad," I muttered.

"Maybe not." Now she just sounded tired. "But if you give him a chance, you might find out he's not so bad."

FRIDAY, MARCH 1

"WE SHOULD BRANCH out," Nathan announced at lunch. His eyes widened behind his thick glasses. "Do some new things."

"Branch out?" Josh asked, as if Nathan spoke in a foreign language. I shot Mark a glance and bit into a salty French fry, intrigued. This kind of comment didn't usually come from Nathan.

Nathan nodded, and his voice raised a few octaves. "Yeah. Time's running out."

"Running out for what?" Mark asked in a quiet voice.

"To make an impact at Heritage. Make it count."

"Make it count?" I asked, as I munched on another fry.

"Come on. This is our senior year."

"Yep. Last I checked." I smirked at Nathan.

"*Senior* year," he said.

"So what?"

Nathan sighed and picked at the green beans on his plate with his plastic fork. He swirled them around as he spoke, making sure all of us could hear him in the loud lunchroom. "It's already March. We only have three months to go, and then school will be out."

"Can't wait for that," I muttered.

Nathan shot me a disapproving look. "Whatever. You're going to regret acting like this."

"No, I'm not," I said, before taking a bite of hamburger, with a crusty wheat bun. "Not going to regret it at all."

"What the hell is wrong with you?"

"There's nothing wrong with me; nothing at all. Except this place." I said, with a smile.

Nathan rolled his eyes. "Jesus, Geoff, you are so sarcastic sometimes."

"Yeah, maybe," I admitted. "But that's just the way I am."

Nathan put down his fork, and locked eyes with me. "Well, it's getting really fucking annoying."

Josh, Mark and I gaped at Nathan. He never cursed. Never. It just wasn't his style. Plus, Nathan sounded way more serious than he had in a long time. As we all stared at him, he continued. "Seriously Geoff, your attitude these days is really shitty."

I held up my now empty hands. My right index finger had some mustard on it, which I ignored. "What the fuck? I don't have an attitude."

"Yeah, you do." Nathan paused to gather his words, then pressed onward with his verbal assault. "A shitty one. I'm getting really sick of it."

"Oh yeah?"

"Yep."

"Where is this coming from?"

Nathan rolled his eyes. "You might think we can't see it, but it's all over you. You act like you're so bored with life here at Heritage, like you're better than everyone else, and like you can't wait to leave all this behind." He paused, and sized me up. "And you're always just assuming things about people. And being a douchebag."

A glance from Nathan to my other friends showed me the truth. Josh and Mark wouldn't look at me, and I knew they agreed with him. Deep inside, I had to admit Nathan had made a good point, but I didn't want to admit that. So I just narrowed my eyes. "What the fuck do you want me to do about it, then, Nathan?"

Nathan laughed without humor, and it made me more frustrated.

"Seriously, what the fuck do you want me to do about it?"

Once I started cussing, our other friends stared at us, transfixed. Nathan and I might have clashed in the past, but never like this. The stalemate grew with every second that passed. Mark and Josh watched us like they were watching a heavyweight championship boxing match, but they were the only ones. All around us, Heritage High students floated from table to table making weekend plans, laughing about gossip they'd heard in chemistry class, the latest article they'd read in *Maxim* or *Cosmopolitan*, and the latest Snapchat someone had sent them in class on their phone.

"Stop being so critical of everyone," Nathan said. "You're critical because you think your life sucks, and Heritage sucks, and you just want out of here."

"But Heritage does suck." I looked at Mark and Josh. When they didn't back me up right away, I changed my tactic. "Don't you guys think that? It sucks."

Josh put his elbows on the table and looked at both of us. "It kinda sucks. But it's not as bad as I used to think it was."

"Dude, that's because you have a girlfriend now," I said, and then glanced around to see if anyone else had noticed what we were saying. Satisfied they hadn't, I continued. "And you're fucking getting laid."

The color faded from Josh's face, and pooled in his neck. He looked at me like I had just kicked him in the face. "What? How did you know about that?"

I laughed. "I didn't. But I do now." I lifted my chin, satisfied to get confirmation. "So, how is Allison?"

"Come on," Josh said, embarrassed. His words came out fast and breathy. "I don't want to talk about her."

"At least you're getting some," Mark muttered.

Nathan, though, kept his icy stare on me. "See what I'm talking about here? You're being an asshole to everyone." He tipped his head in Josh's direction. "That was a dick move."

"Whatever, we're all friends." I glanced at my friend and my confidence faded. "It's fine, right? I mean, I'm glad things are going well with Allison."

"It's fine. It's whatever. Just shut up about it," Josh replied, but he didn't look at me anymore. He just looked like he wanted lunch to be over. Right away.

"So, what do you want me to do about it?" I asked Nathan, belligerent.

"I want you to fucking get your head out of your ass!" Nathan exclaimed. "You have everything going for you. You're salutatorian, and you're not even trying! And you're going to Virginia. And you can get any girl you want in this school if you want her."

I burst out laughing. "Now, that's where you are totally wrong."

"Stop acting like some kind of angry trollop," Nathan said. "And yes, you can get any girl."

"I think he wants Laine Phillips." Mark snickered, and Josh laughed some, too.

"Whatever. I can't get any girl."

Nathan rolled his eyes up to the ceiling. Sarcasm dripped from his voice. "Should I describe you to yourself? Your big eyes? That sandy brown and blonde hair?" His voice became high-pitched as he started ticking off my physical features. "That rock hard chest? That smile?"

"Shut up."

"All those hours you spend working out in your room?"

"Shut up!"

Nathan wasn't wrong, though. I'd lost fifteen pounds in three months.

"You know, not everyone in this school is against you, Geoff," Nathan said, undaunted by my pleas. "People want to like you, but you won't let them."

"They all call me Geoff Megadeth," I replied. "They don't like me."

"Why do you care? Why not just own it, instead of trying to fight it?"

"Whatever." I bit into what remained of my burger. "Easy for you to say."

Nathan nodded. "Yeah. It is. And I'm tired of it. We have just a few months of school left. Nothing to lose. We need to do something awesome. Make this shit count."

"Okay," I said after I swallowed my bite. "So what is

this? Some sort of challenge??"

"Yeah, Geoff, that's what it is. A challenge."

"Okay," I said, aware I was talking out of my ass, but too stubborn to go back on it now. "I'll take it. How do you want to prove to me that you're going to stop being a douchebag?" I thought about it. "I think you should do something you've never done before."

He considered it. "Okay. We have AP English, and the reading guide for *Macbeth* is due. I have mine in my locker, but I won't hand it in. I'll just skip class."

"That's 10 percent of our grade," Mark pointed out.

"So what?" Nathan glanced at him, unfettered. "I've never skipped class before. I bet I can do it, and get away with it."

"What . . . what are you . . . where are you going to go instead?" I asked.

He shrugged. "Does it matter? To my car, I guess, to listen to music. Go home. Or maybe I'll just go to the library."

"That really a good idea?" Mark asked.

Nathan and I ignored him and eyed each other, still locked in the argument.

"Okay," I said, convinced. "So now, what do I have to do?"

Nathan gave me a Cheshire cat grin. "You have to ask Laine out. Here. In the lunchroom."

The air around me thickened. "No way. She's still dating Evan."

I glanced in the direction of the table where I knew Laine sat. She did, as always, have a smile on her face, and she picked at her daily salad while one of her friends told the latest gossip about boys in school. It was as if all of

Heritage spun on an axle around her, while she maintained a quiet serenity—the reigning Greek goddess of the school.

Mark shook his head. "That's not what I heard. She and Evan are on the out. At least, for right now."

"They are?" I asked, puzzled. I didn't know about any of this. Why didn't I? Nothing about Laine got past me. *Nothing.* So why hadn't I heard about this?

"I think it just happened," Mark said, answering the question in my head. "That's what I heard some girls saying in Spanish class this morning. I guess Evan broke up with her."

"Really?" As soon as the word came out, I knew my question sounded too hopeful, too eager. But I couldn't help myself. "Is she upset?"

Matt shrugged.

Nathan slapped his hands together, and the tray of food in front of him rattled. "There. That settles it. She's single. You have to ask her out."

"Now?"

"Yeah, asshole." He smiled. "Do it now."

"Right now?" I gulped.

"Yep. Do it right now. And if you do, I'll skip class. Deal?"

I took about thirty seconds to gather my wits as I considered Nathan's challenge. The whole time he stared at me with a sly, almost sarcastic, grin, as if he knew he was sending me to my death. At the very least, this teetered on the edge of an outcome I couldn't guess. Who cared if Laine sent me anonymous Valentine's Day chocolates, and friended me on social media? And what did a couple of stolen conversations matter? The rest of the Heritage student body had no idea we'd ever talked. Once I got up and walked over to her, everyone would know. Everyone. Half the senior class sat in the cafeteria at that very moment, and even more freshmen, sophomores, and juniors filled out the rest of the tables.

In other words, I'd hear about this, no matter what.

"You have to do it," Nathan repeated. "You do it, and like I said, I'll skip the next class. Okay?"

Something twisted inside my stomach. I eyed Laine, who looked finished with whatever vegetables she had on her tray. She'd be getting up from the table soon. "Deal," I said.

Mark sucked in a long breath. "Oh, wow. This is going to be good."

"I'm so glad I didn't go off campus for lunch with Allison today," Josh said.

I shut out my friends and focused only on Laine. She laughed with her friends and then suddenly stood up from the table, her tray in her hand. No one else got up, and she sauntered away from the table toward the tray return counter at the far end of the room. As she walked, I saw how guys sitting at tables all over the cafeteria followed her with their eyes. I wasn't the only person in the room with a crush on Laine Phillips.

But of course, I knew that.

Pulling together every nerve in my body, I pushed back my metal chair and stood up with my tray. If I hurried, I'd manage to catch her before she walked away from the tray return, but that also meant the entire cafeteria would have a direct line of sight to me. Oh, well. No choice. Time to navigate the high school jungle. Time to man up.

Right, then.

With a smile to my friends, I turned and made my way to the tray return. Laine had her back to me as I walked up, carefully sorting what remained of her lunch into trash and recycle bins. Other students clanged around doing the same thing. I put my tray on a waiting metal table, and tapped her on the shoulder. "Hey, Laine."

She whirled around, her eyes wide, and then she grinned at me. "Geoff, hey. What's up?"

A sophomore wearing a long sleeved T-shirt with a no-name band on it shot me a confused look. I nodded in his direction, and turned back to Laine.

"So, um, did you have a nice lunch?"

"It was okay." She shrugged. "Just the usual salad."

"Yeah, I hate salads."

"Me, too." Her eyes smiled at me. "They keep me thin. And, well, you know, I don't want to get fat."

"You don't have to worry about that."

She looked away from me. "Easy for you to say." When her eyes met mine again though, any trace of whatever bothered her had disappeared. "You look nice today, Geoff."

I glanced down, shocked. "I do?"

"Come on. You know you do."

I shook my head in disbelief. She thought I looked nice? Really? "Um, thanks."

"You look hot. You've lost weight, right?"

"Well... um... yeah..." The words slid out of my mouth slower than peanut butter coming out of a jar. "I mean...I've been working out...."

She laughed, and I immediately searched for what to say next. The word "hot" thundered through my head over and over. Nathan had dared me to ask out the girl of my dreams, and I'd seized the challenge, but now, as I stood in front of her, I couldn't think of a suave way to do it, especially not now that she'd noticed me. So I said the first few words that came to my mind.

"Listen, Laine, um, I was wondering what you were . . . um . . . what you were doing this weekend." It came out as a statement, but should have been a question.

"I don't know. I have cheer practice this afternoon, and then after that . . ."

She trailed off as a few other students stopped what they were doing to watch us talk. In fact, over my shoulder, I saw a couple of people at various tables turn their heads in our direction. Some of them had confused looks, while others gave me the kind of disdainful stare I had seen many times on Blake and Bruce's faces. As I'd expected.

"Cheer practice sounds fun." What the hell was I saying? I sounded like an idiot.

She grinned. "Yeah, it is. It will be. Monica and I are supposed to be working on some new routines."

"New routines? Sounds amazing."

Once I said it, I could have kicked myself in the face. What was I thinking? I didn't like cheerleading. I didn't care about it at all. Recover. I needed to recover. Immediately.

"Well, if you aren't too busy, I thought we might do something this weekend. Maybe Saturday?"

A fat junior must have heard me ask this, because she burst out laughing as she placed her tray on the metal table and dumped the rest of her soup into the trashcan.

"This weekend?" Laine scrunched up her face as she

thought about it. "Yeah, I'm free Saturday night." She leaned into me, and the familiar bubble gum smell drifted up my nose. "I guess you know I broke it off with Evan."

"Yeah, I heard," I said, still seething that I'd found that information out from Mark.

"He's not . . . we . . . we just needed a break." She turned her head, and looked away again.

"I'm sorry," I said, even though I wasn't at all. I hated Evan so much. He always loomed over everything, like a bad rash, or a bruise. "So . . . um . . . do you want me to just send you a message on Facebook, or something?"

Why was it so hard to do this? Oh, right. Because it was her. Jesus, she was nothing but nice to me, but I never managed to make these conversations sound the way I wanted. I needed to fix that.

"Why don't you call me?" she said, her attention on me again.

"Well . . . okay . . ." I replied, and then faltered again. My right hand started to shake.

"Here's my number—seven . . . three . . . one . . ."

"Wait, I don't have my phone. It's in my locker," I interrupted, but inside I was kind of glad I didn't. My hand shook so hard I couldn't have held it.

She grinned. "Okay. I'll message you my number on Facebook." She took a step backward. "And you'll call me, right?"

"Yeah," I said. "I'll call you." I didn't add that I would call her every day if she wanted me to.

"Great. Talk to you later."

She turned, and flounced back to her table. My eyes fell on Mark, Nathan and Josh. They all stared at me, wide-eyed, as if I had the answer to the location of Jimmy

Hoffa's dead body. I waited until I sat back down at the table to say anything. By then, anticipation had her own seat at our table.

"So," I said, "she has cheerleading practice tonight."

"Oh, man," Josh muttered. "I knew she would turn you down."

I burst out laughing, still in some disbelief myself. "She didn't. She said she'd do something Saturday night."

Nathan's fork clattered against his tray. "She did?"

"Yeah. She did." I leaned back in my chair, and folded my arms. "So, looks like you're missin' that class."

"Damn it," Nathan said. "I thought for sure you'd chicken out."

He should have known better than to make a bet with me. I didn't like to lose.

Josh's mouth hung open, but Mark found some words. "Dude, you are absolutely my hero right now."

By the time fifth period switched into sixth, I'd been asked about my date with Laine forty times. I counted. It started with the stony glare Evan gave me in World Cultures class, where he proceeded to fart more than usual and seemed to aim it at my face. Kids stopped me in the hallway between classes. They taunted me under their breath as I walked down a row to my seat in class. They spoke in hushed voices, and greeted me with the kind of cold stare that only comes from classmates who think you've done something you shouldn't have. In short, they wanted me to know how much I had overstepped my boundaries.

I ignored it all as I took notes and wrote down homework assignments. Fuck them. Fuck the whole school. They could all go to hell on a one-way ticket.

After class, Blake and Bruce waited for me by the car in the chilly, stale winter air. I'll admit, I walked a little slower than I should have down the sidewalk in front of the school, and across the street to the student parking lot. I liked making them wait, and on Fridays they relied on me to get home.

"You're such an asshole," Bruce muttered as I walked up to them with a big, leisurely grin on my face. His cheeks were flushed from the cold chap of the final days of winter.

"I'm the asshole?" I said in mock protest, as I unlocked the car with the key fob.

"You could have walked a little faster, couldn't you?" Bruce narrowed his eyes at me. "Or was that too much for you?"

"He was probably daydreaming about his nonexistent upcoming date with Laine," Blake said to his brother.

I kept my face serene. "Well, the car is unlocked now. Don't you want to get in?"

Both of the twins did, of course. They didn't speak to me again until after I pulled the car out of the parking lot and turned onto North Robert Road, the long main drag that took us right by Heritage High School and the other big landmarks in town—*big* being a relative term.

"So," Blake said, his voice thick with innuendo, "we heard you took a little gamble today in the lunchroom."

I said nothing. I just kept on driving, with both hands on the wheel.

"Laine Phillips," Bruce said, picking up the cues from

his brother. "Wow. Aim high."

My hands tightened on the leather wheel, but again, I said nothing as I stopped at a four-way stop about four blocks from the school. The stares and whispered comments from the rest of the school had been more than enough warning about this conversation.

"Dude, the least you can do is turn up the radio," Blake complained. He reached over from his place in the front passenger seat and twisted the dial. Jay-Z's voice blasted through the speakers of the car. He raised his voice. "Anyway. Laine. Interesting."

"Not that interesting."

I drove the car through the intersection, and past a few quiet streets lined with brick homes built in the 1940s. I liked these houses because they reminded me of the one I grew up in, back before Dad got sick and before Mom "reconnected" with David. And before, of course, I got stuck living with the two trollops who'd hated me all through elementary school, and who now loved to pick on me for being smarter than them. Six months to go; at the most. Six months to go, and I'd be away from this snobby little town, the terrible twins, and a suburban mindset I could never understand. By the fall, I'd live in Charlottesville, Virginia, and study at one of the best schools in the country. Six months wasn't really that long.

Even though sometimes it seemed like six months would take longer to pass than ten years.

"She doesn't like you that way," Bruce said, as we passed St. Margaret's Catholic Church. "She doesn't. You're not her type."

"Who is her type?"

Bruce snorted. "Not you. Not anyone like you."

"She just feels bad for you," Blake added as I turned the car onto Ammunition Ridge. "And she's too nice to say anything. That's how Laine Phillips is. She's too nice."

Chapter Seven

SATURDAY, MARCH 2

I REHEARSED THE phone call twelve times before I made it: five times in the shower, four in front of the bathroom mirror, twice while I ran on the treadmill in the workout room, and once more as I scrubbed the tiles on the kitchen floor on Saturday morning.

True to her promise, Laine had sent me her phone number; she sent it right after class on Friday. The 3:25 time stamp made me grin. She did want to hang out. Blake, Bruce, and those asshats at my school were wrong. Not that I really expected them to be right. They didn't have many brain cells, and struggled to name all fifty states on the map.

Sitting on my bed, I dialed her number and then counted the rings: *One. Two. Three. Four.* Then, just when I thought she'd send me to voicemail, she picked up the phone.

"Hey, hello?"

I pulled the phone to my ear. "Laine. Hey."

"What's up?" She sounded out of breath.

"Are you, are you okay?" I lay back on the bed and willed my heart to stop pounding, and for thoughts about how she'd look naked to get out of my head. *Focus.* I needed to focus. I couldn't let her sexy voice distract me, no matter how much I wanted it to.

"Yeah, I'm fine. I just finished a hot yoga class."

"Hot yoga?"

She laughed. "Yeah, ninety minutes doing yoga in a studio at two hundred degrees. So I don't get fat."

"Like I told you before, you don't need to worry about that."

When she laughed again, as if she didn't believe me, I put my hand over my eyes. I needed to get this conversation back on track right away. This wasn't how I had envisioned it would start.

"Listen, so, um, I thought if you still wanted to hang out that might be kind of fun," I said after a moment, hoping I didn't sound too urgent or desperate.

"Yeah, of course I want to," she replied. "What were you, um, what were you thinking? A movie, or something like that?"

"Well, no." I paused. "I had something a little different in mind. Do you like Mexican?"

"Yeah."

"Six?"

"Okay." She hesitated. "Wait. Geoff?"

"What?"

"What should I wear?"

"Oh, it's just a casual place. It's not dressy." I rushed my words. I didn't want her to back out now that I had my plan in motion. This had to work. *Had to.*

"Great," she said after a minute. "I guess I'll see you tonight."

"I'll pick you up at six. You live on Halloway, right?"

She laughed again. "How do you know so much about me, Geoff?"

I laughed right along with her, and changed the subject as fast as I could.

Laine and her parents lived in a small white colonial on Halloway in the center of Robert Hill. It had a detached two-car garage, a large tree in the front yard, and a red front door.

Halloway was just around the corner from Kentwood Elementary, a tan brick building where I'd spent the first six years of school getting my face shoved in gravel, missing kick balls during gym class, and beating my classmates in geography bees.

She waited for me on the wide front porch, and stood up when I pulled the car in next to the curb. She had on a dressy trench coat and one of those huge puffy skirts that reminded me of a ballerina tutu. I gulped when I saw it. First, because as she walked down the sidewalk, she looked like she was walking the runway for a fashion show. Second, because it made me wonder if she considered this a date.

Of course, I considered it a date.

I did. Before I left the house, I tucked three hundred bucks of my money into my wallet, spritzed some Woodland cologne on my chest, and popped two breath mints, just in case. As she walked toward the car, I wondered if maybe she'd done the same.

That thought made my hands start to shake.

"Hey," she said, as she pulled open the car door. I would have gotten out to help her in, but she did it so fast it caught me off guard. "You look nice."

"Yeah," I replied as she got into the car. "So do you. You really do." I pulled the car away from the curb, and started down the street. The whole time, I had to focus on my hands to keep them from shaking so badly. She couldn't see how nervous she made me; it would kill the date before it even began. That is, if this was a date. I wasn't so sure about that.

"I thought we could go downtown," I choked out, as I stopped the car at the stop sign on the corner of Halloway. I glanced at her out of the corner of my eye, trying to gauge her reaction to my idea. "How about Nada?"

"Isn't that place expensive?"

"Nah. It's not that bad."

"I've heard it is."

"Trust me, it's not."

She gave me a sideways glance. "Don't we have to have a reservation?"

"We don't need one," I said, with a confident glance her way.

"We don't?"

"Nope. Nathan's bother works as the sous chef at the place. We've got connections, Laine." I leaned back in the seat, willing myself to relax. So what if this was Laine? We were just hanging out. Two friends headed out on a Saturday night to downtown Cincinnati. That was all.

Laine raised her hand up as we pulled out on to I-471. "What. Wait. What are you listening to?"

"Oh, it's um . . . nothing . . ." I'd turned down the radio out of instinct when I pulled up to her house. Ever since the kids at school had made a big deal about my Megadeth band T-shirt, conversation about music with the other kids at school had been off-limits. They didn't need more ammunition to make fun of me.

"No, it's not nothing, Geoff." She reached over and turned the dial up on the console. The Silverplate Band's wailing blared through the speakers. "Is this the Lithium station on XM?"

"Well . . . um . . . yeah."

She held up her hand, and closed her eyes. "I love this song, Geoff."

"You do?"

"You say my love . . . can't buy what you want . . . Girl, I know you need me more . . ." She kept her eyes closed as she sang the second verse. "You think you can keep on going . . . acting like you don't care . . . but I strongly doubt it . . ."

My eyes widened in shock. She really did know the words. And her voice wasn't so bad, either.

"Come on, Geoff," she said during a guitar solo. "You gotta sing with me."

"Okay," I said, and then waited for the chorus. "Yyyyyyoooooouuuuu . . . never loved meeeeee . . ."

She laughed when I joined in, but then she kept on singing. Together, we belted the lyrics as I drove the car across the bridge and into Ohio. She even tossed in some air guitar. God, this was one confident girl, and she had mad fake music skills.

Sexy.

"So, you like nineties alternative rock," I said once we turned onto 5th Street, the heart of downtown.

We passed nightclubs just opening up, throngs of people on their way to parties, bachelorettes ready for a night out, and college kids headed to the bars that lined Cincinnati's Restaurant Row. I always liked the change I felt once I was in the heart of the city and not on the suburban streets of Robert Hill. Something about the bustle of the city made my spirit come alive. If I ever lived in Cincinnati as an adult, I would make sure I lived downtown. I knew that much.

She shrugged. "Who doesn't?"

"Well, I didn't think most people did . . . considering we weren't born for most of it—"

"Who cares?" She laughed. "My brother loves music. He runs a guitar store up in Oxford, and he made me some playlists last year. I liked it, so I listen to it."

"I just took you for—"

Her laughter cut me off again. "Whatever. When are you going to stop judging people, Geoff?"

"Let's order, like, five different things, and try them all," Laine said as we looked over the menus.

We sat at a table near Nada's large glass windows. From our spot, we had a view of the patio and the street. I also had a view of the rest of the restaurant, if I looked past Laine. Men in business suits mingled with women in short dresses, over cocktails at the bar. Large groups of friends laughed at tables near us. Everyone in this restaurant could have come out of a magazine for pretty people, and most of them treated a stop here as pre-game for something else. We were by far the youngest people in the room. I hid my smile as I wondered if it pissed the waiter off to get a table with two teenagers. Oh well, I had the money. And I'd waited for this.

Laine dipped a large tortilla chip in the small bowl of spicy salsa on the table. "Hmm. I think we should get the guac. I love guac."

"Okay," I said. "There's order number one. What else?"

We settled on the guacamole, Mexican mac 'n' cheese, chicken taquitos, carnitas tacos, and boca fries. When the food came out, it covered the table so much so that I worried moving one plate might knock something on the floor. The food looked like something a binge-eater would dream about. I knew I was hungry, but was she?

Yep, she was.

She ate the chicken taquitos with gusto, and didn't wait to dive into the boca fries and carnitas tacos. We didn't say much to each other beyond exclamation about how delicious the fries and the Mexican mac 'n' cheese tasted. I think this was the best meal I'd ever had. Really. There was something magical about watching the hottest girl in school devour a meal that had a couple of thousand calories in it. Salads, be damned.

"That was amazing." Laine smiled as a staffer took away the now empty plates. "I haven't eaten like that in a while."

"Yeah," I replied. "I mean, I can eat that way, for sure, but it's awesome to do it here."

"No wonder I keep on hearing about this place. I mean, I know there are other places, but this one I always wanted to go to."

"Yep." I looked around the room. "Downtown is pretty cool. I like it a lot."

She leaned back in her chair, and pushed her half empty glass of Diet Coke away from her. "I wonder what it's going to be like next year, at Xavier."

"Me, too," I said. "Charlottesville looks fun, but I just don't know what to expect."

She raised an eyebrow, and tilted her head. "Wait a second. You're not going to Gateway Tech? You're not following Mr. Henderson's advice?"

"No way. He's just crazy." I put up one hand.

"You're not salutatorian yet." She laughed. "Who knows? Someone might unseat you." She dropped her eyes down at the table, and a sly smile spread across her face. "Like me, maybe."

"I hope you do, Laine."

She looked up again. "I'm just kidding."

"Seriously. I hope you do." I broke her gaze and looked at the crowd in the restaurant, but didn't really see anything or anyone. "Maybe you'll knock off Nichole Reese, too." My mouth contorted as I thought about her. "Yeah, I'd like that a lot.'"

"All Nichole does is sit at home and study," Laine pointed out. "Not that she talks to me, or anything. She's kinda . . . mean." Her eyes shifted, and I realized that fact bothered her. Now it was my turn to sit back, stunned.

"Wait. You think she's mean?"

Laine nodded. "Yeah. She's mean. She acts like my friends are all idiots. You should hear the things she says to Jillian. It's really horrible."

I might have agreed with Nichole there. Jillian *was* kind of an idiot. That girl once told me she didn't know if hydrogen was on the Periodic Table. Still, it had never occurred to me that the popular kids in school might have been as bothered by bullying and mean kids as the rest of us. "Well, I'm glad I'm not the only one who thinks she's awful."

"She really is."

The waiter returned with the check, and I paid the $60 bill with no complaint. As I did, Laine shifted her view to the people outside the restaurant, and a wistful look came over her face. "I can't wait to get out of Robert Hill."

"Me too."

"People put you in boxes there," she muttered. "They try to make you something you're not. Like, they have your life decided for you already. Who you're going to be. What you're going to do. All of it."

"Especially if you are someone like me."

"No, Geoff," she said. "Especially if you're someone like me. And some people think they can just . . ." Her phone buzzed and she looked down.. She glanced at it, and then shook her head, as if shutting down whatever the person on the other end wanted. "Whatever. What do you want to do? Do you want to walk around some?"

"Sure, I guess." I stood up from the table. "Do you want to walk over to Fountain Square, or something?"

She grinned. "Let's go for a drive."

About fifteen minutes later, I pulled the car into a parking spot at the Eden Park overlook, a small park with benches that lined a stone walkway and retaining wall. Laine's directions had taken us through Downtown, and up the winding hills to Mt. Adams, a glamorous and expensive neighborhood full of young professionals and homes sandwiched together in competition for the best view of the hills around Cincinnati, and then finally through the rambling beauty of Eden Park to the overlook. The whole time we drove, we sang more songs from the Lithium station on XM satellite radio. By the time I threw the car into park we'd sung Radiohead, Nirvana, and Pearl Jam. I should have caught it in a video on my iPhone.

"This is my favorite place in the city," Laine said, as we hopped out of the car and walked across the parking lot to the benches that lined the overlook. She pulled her coat closer to her, to ward off the March chill as we took seats on the cold metal. "My absolute favorite."

"Why is that?" I sat next to her, but not too close. I didn't want to overstep any boundaries.

"I like how you can see the bends in the river from this angle." She gestured to the Ohio River which fanned out on both sides, leaving the tip of Northern Kentucky in front of us. Robert Hill lay in the distance, high on one of the hills, while Dayton, Bellevue, Ft. Thomas and Newport bustled below us, all at the banks of the river and lit up with thousands of streetlights.

"Nice night," I said, as we both took in the view. She kept her eyes on the city, but mine darted back and forth between the gorgeous city and the gorgeousness of her. "Really nice view."

She leaned back on the bench, stretched out her legs,

and crossed them at the ankles. "I come up here a lot."

"A lot?"

"Mm-hmm." Her voice relaxed.. "When I want to think. It's peaceful."

"How did you know about this place?"

"My parents brought me up here when I was a kid. Mom really likes flowers, so we'd come up to the park a lot and go to the conservatory. Sometimes we stopped here, so I always knew about it."

"I've never been up here before. Not that I can remember."

"Really?" She turned to me with a small smile on her lips. "It's a great place to think about things. Like what I want to do with my life."

"What do you want to do? I mean, besides the fashion thing."

Forget the view. All my attention was on her now, and I couldn't think of a better place for it to be. God, this gorgeous girl made my head spin, but I didn't want to stop it. I wanted the ride to never, ever end.

"Get out of Robert Hill." She chuckled.

"But you're the princess of Robert Hill." It came out with a sarcastic tone, so I softened my words. "Everyone loves you at school. They'll always love you."

"Not everyone loves me. And Princess. I hate how people call me that." She wrinkled her nose, then broke her gaze with me and looked at the view of the river. "It's a stupid nickname."

I sat back, surprised. She'd had that nickname for as long as I'd known her. "You hate it?"

"Yeah. It's not me. It's like, people just say it because they think I have some kind of easy life, and I don't. Stuff bothers me, too." She giggled, as if she knew the punch line to a joke no one else had heard. "And I think some kids just say that because they kinda hate me."

"Well, they call me Geoff Megadeth."

She laughed. "Creative, right?"

I shook my head, disgusted. "Just because I wore a Megadeth T-shirt a couple of times in the fifth grade. I mean, really."

"Whatever. They are so small-minded." A pause. "Have you ever noticed how people in Robert Hill grow up and go off to college, and the come right back here and never leave?" She popped one shoulder. "My cousin did that, and I'm just like, why?"

"Yep. That's how it is. Everyone's like that. I'm sure Blake and Bruce will be that way, too."

"Blake and Bruce. Do you like them?"

I threw up one hand. "Sure I do. Everything about them is great. Best stepbrothers a guy could ask for."

"Whatever." She grinned at me. "I know you hate them."

"Hate is a really strong word. I wouldn't want . . ." I thought about it. "Okay, maybe you're right."

"Blake and Bruce aren't really all that great of guys, trust me. Earlier in the year, Monica had a crush on Blake, and she tried to do what she could to get with him. And they weren't . . . they're very—"

The sound of her phone cut off her words. She fished around in the front pocket of her purple purse, and when she looked at the screen, she frowned. I knew right then who it was: Evan. It had be Evan. Damn it. She stood up, and walked away from the bench, but I still heard her end of the conversation.

"Hello? Hi . . . yes . . . no . . . I'm out right now . . . You did? . . . Listen, I don't want to talk about that . . . well . . . I mean . . . Look, I'm sorry . . . Okay . . . I know . . . Please . . . Yep. I'll be there. Half hour."

When she turned back to me and threw her phone in her pocket, I stood up from the bench. Even in the winter darkness, I saw the change in her body language: hunched shoulders, an averted gaze, and the nervous way her fingers pulled on the hem of her skirt. I didn't need to ask my next question, but I did anyway.

"Let me guess. Evan?'

"I need to go home," she said, sounding urgent and unsettled. "Yeah, like right now. Is that okay?"

"I guess," I said, not bothering to hide my sadness as I walked to the car. "No problem." The magic of our night had disappeared fast, like an early morning mist on the Ohio River. Nothing was the same now, and we couldn't get those few stolen moments back. She followed me, and we got into the car without another word to each other. The spell had broken, and I knew it.

Chapter eight

MONDAY, MARCH 4TH

SHE DIDN'T HAVE to tell me anything. I heard it in the hallway right after I walked through the door front doors of Heritage that morning. Underclassmen whispered it in conversations by their lockers, and shot me pitiful looks, as if they'd sized me up and decided that I'd been the biggest fool to ever grace the halls of our suburban school. I caught a couple of kids mid-laugh, as if they didn't realize I'd walk right by them, and then felt embarrassed that I did. When I strode up to Nathan and Josh just before first period, they wouldn't look me in the eye.

"What? What is it?" I only asked it to start the conversation. I already knew what they would say.

"Nothing," Josh said, but his bright voice seemed fake. I knew right away that he had something more to say, but that he couldn't figure out how to tell me. "Nothin' at all, dude."

"Come on." Nathan socked him in the arm. "We're

his friends. We should tell him."

"Tell me what?" I shifted my backpack from one shoulder to the other.

Josh looked away from me. "It's Laine. She's back with . . ."

"She's back with Evan?" In my head, I sounded flip. I hoped that's how I came across to them. "They got back together?"

"Yeah, they did." Nathan clapped me on my shoulder. "You okay about it?"

"That's not the only thing, though," Josh said, raising his voice. "They aren't . . . well . . . everyone is sayin' . . ."

"Saying what?" I tapped my foot.

"They're saying she stood you up. That you showed up at her house, and she was there with Evan, and that you looked stupid because you had flowers and thought she would actually want to go out with you. And that Evan had to tell you the truth."

I sucked in a hard breath. They knew this would hurt me, and it did. This could only have come from Evan himself. Laine wouldn't spread a stupid rumor like that, but Evan would. What an asshole. Why did everybody act like this guy had been crowned king of Robert Hill?

"Nice," I replied. I chose my next words with the precision of a surgeon. I needed to hide the pain I felt from them, and fast. "Just so you guys know, we did go on a date. And it was great, until she took a phone call from that jerk-off."

"A date?" Josh asked.

"Yep."

Nathan and Josh exchanged glances as the bell rang.

"Okay," Josh said. "Whatever you say. Just wanted

you to know what people were saying about you."

I answered with a fake laugh, and motioned for us to walk the rest of the way to class. Since when had I really cared what people thought? Well, I did care, but I also knew where I stood with most of them. My classmates didn't understand me, and never would. They thought of me as some kind of smart geek who did nothing but study, as he treaded water somewhere in the middle tier of Heritage High's social hierarchy. Whatever. I'd be out of there in less than three months, anyway, and on my way to UVA while they floated around wondering what to do next with their lives.

As for Laine? I had been an idiot once again. What I thought was a date with the hottest girl in school had turned out to be just a distraction for her. She didn't think it was a date, not in the least, and I should have known that. It was just what I deserved for thinking I could have someone like her.

I squared my shoulders and walked into class, three steps behind Josh and Nathan. Everyone else had taken their seats, so we made an entrance.

"Nice of you boys to join us," Mr. Langston said from behind his podium. "It's not like we have a major test to take in just over two months."

"Sorry, Mr. Langston," Nathan muttered, making it clear he spoke for all of us.

"Turn to page 295 in your text," Mr. Langston said to the rest of the class. He clapped his hands. "Wake up, everyone. Every second of the next few weeks count. No more sleepwalking through Mondays."

I threw my book bag down next to my desk. As I did, my eyes caught Laine's gaze. She bit her lower lip, and her eyes looked bigger than usual. "I'm sorry," she mouthed after a moment.

All I did was shrug and slide into the desk. I could have been mad or upset, but I didn't feel like it. I just wanted to stay numb and make it through the rest of high school. Whatever.

TUESDAY, MARCH 12

JOSH HAD WIDE eyes and a snide smile when he set his tray down at our table for lunch. In fact, a red blush rimmed his round face, and I wondered for a half second if he had some kind of strange disease. I hadn't heard anything about him getting sick, though.

"Dude," Nathan said, in between bites of his apple. "You look weird."

"Do I?" Josh replied as he sat down. His eyes danced, the same way a lot of people's did when they got the Christmas present they'd wanted, or found $20 dollars in their pocket. I'd seen Josh excited before, but not often like this.

"What's up?" I asked. "Something's up."

Josh glanced at the other tables close to ours. Around us, students did the usual. They chattered about their day, and ate lunch without paying attention to us.

"I had to go to the nurse's office this morning because I thought I was getting a migraine in Spanish," Josh said, after he was satisfied no else wanted to listen to our conversation. "You know. Mom sent up some medication at the beginning of year, and they keep it there."

"Right," I said, prompting Josh to continue his story. He got migraines about three times a year, and we all knew about it. Old news.

"Anyway, when Mrs. Turner went to the get the medicine out of the back, I noticed an open box on the floor by her desk." He bit back a smile. "Know what was in it?"

Nathan sighed, his attention still on his half eaten lunch. "What?"

Josh looked around again as the rest of the bustling lunchroom. "Okay, you guys can't tell anyone." With a dramatic flourish, he reached in to his back pocket, then slowly slid a small red square packet along the edge of the table, letting just enough show so that Mark, Nathan and I would see it.

Nathan's fork fell out of his hand, and clattered onto his tray. "Whoa. Is that what I think it is?"

Mark nodded, and choked on his orange juice.

Josh grinned at all of us. "Yep. It's what you think it is." He leaned in closer to us, and the words tumbled out of his mouth. "It was a whole box of condoms. I have no idea why she had them, but she did. There must have been five hundred in there."

"How many did you take?" I asked.

"I grabbed a handful before she came back in." He nodded at us, as if he wanted to back up what he was saying. "Four of them. One for each of us."

Mark sat back, crossed his arms, and his mouth hung open. He didn't speak for about thirty seconds. "Wow. Man. You are amazing."

"Well done," Nathan said.

"But we don't need them," I pointed out. "We're not getting any."

"Shut up." Josh glared at me. "You might not be getting any, but it won't always be that way. And it's not that way for me."

"Whoa," I said. "Mister Confident. Maybe I'll call Allison over here and tell her you just said that."

"Just take one," Josh said. He fished around in his jeans pocket again, pulled out the other three, and handed one to each of us under the table, as if they were drugs or stolen merchandise. "You'll thank me later."

I stifled my laughter as I put one in my wallet. The way things were going in my life I wouldn't need this stupid condom for at least five years. By then, it would probably just be an expired shred of latex.

She caught me at my locker after the last bell. I didn't get my stuff fast enough, and she found me there, switching out books, about five minutes after the last bell sounded.

"So. I guess you heard," she said, as she leaned up against the locker next to mine and bit her lip. "I mean, it's been all over the place for the last week."

I slammed my locker door shut. "What? About you and Evan? Yeah, I heard."

"I felt so bad about that Saturday. I shouldn't have taken that call, but I didn't know what to do, and his text said it was important."

"Whatever," I said, as I scooped my backpack up off the floor. "He's your boyfriend. It happens."

She nodded. "I had a really fun time with you that

night. It was great."

"Me, too." By now I had the backpack on both of my shoulders, so I started my walk to the car. She followed me, her small booted feet working overtime to keep up with my longer strides. "But you know, it was all in my imagination, right?"

"You've heard the rumors?" When I nodded my head, yes, she continued. "I hate people sometimes. Listen, it's not what you—"

"You really like him, don't you?" I stopped walking just after we made it out of Heritage's front door, and she almost ran into me. "Evan. You really like him. Because you didn't seem like you did when we were over in Mt. Adams at the overlook."

"Yeah—about that phone call . . . Evan had some stuff going on, and I didn't want to make it worse. He'd already send me a bunch of text message about it, and I felt so bad about ignoring him." Her eyes shifted away from mine. "So I had to go."

"Whatever. You don't have to make up excuses."

"He needs me, Geoff." She turned her head. "And he's been my boyfriend for so long. It's what I'm used to. And what everyone expects."

"You don't have to do what everyone expects all the time, Laine." I reached over and turned her gaze back to mine with a swipe of my finger. "And look—Saturday was a friend thing, right? Two friends, having fun."

Lying to myself like this made things easier. If we were just friends, then it didn't hurt so much that she'd ditched me for Evan. Friends didn't get hurt when someone got back together with their boyfriend, even if they didn't like that boyfriend. Friends just carried on as if nothing happened.

"Friends." She said the word slowly. "Yeah. I guess."

"We'll still talk," I said. "Of course we will."

"Sure," she said, but her voice sounded hollow.

In fact, she sounded about as convinced as I felt—which was not very.

Chapter nine

FRIDAY, MARCH 22

BLAKE, BRUCE AND I settled into a tenuous routine by the end of March. We gathered around the breakfast table in the house three times a week for a two-hour tutoring lesson on Mondays, Wednesdays and Fridays. They listened to me about 45 percent of the time. Most of the sessions consisted of them rolling their eyes, and making the usual snide comments. I found out a few things about them, though.

Blake liked English, but he didn't want his brother to know. In fact, I suspected he got bad grades on tests just to please his twin, who had a hard time reading above the fifth grade level. Bruce did better in Science and Math.

They didn't like each other all the time, either. In fact, they hated the endless comparisons to each other almost as much as they hated the fact that my mother had married their father, and ended any hope of reconciliation for their parents.

The best part of all, though, was how much my intelligence threatened them. They hated that. Once I found that out, I used it to my advantage in any way I could.

Like today.

"So," I said, as the two of them struggled to write down a readable synopsis of *The Great Gatsby*. They had a test coming up on the material the following Monday. "Tell me one of the most famous quotes from that book."

Bruce looked up from his notebook, and blinked at me. "Quote?"

"Sure." I leaned back against my chair and calmly took a sip of the Diet Coke in front of me. "That book is full of them."

"I don't remember any quotes," Bruce said after a few seconds, and this comment didn't surprise me.

"Here's one," I said, after another swallow of Diet Coke. "*Her voice was full of money.*"

Blank stares answered my words.

"And another. *Rich girls don't marry poor boys, Jay Gatsby.*" I tapped my fingers on the table. I liked F.Scott more than most kids in my class, and it annoyed me that my stepbrothers couldn't see anything about the deeper meaning of his words. "Think that one is true? F. Scott Fitzgerald sure did."

Blake snickered. "It's true in Robert Hill." He paused. "Well, at least at Heritage. Not that anyone's getting married. But when it comes to dating, yeah."

"You guys date whoever you want."

"But that's just it." Blake cleared his throat. "There are certain girls I can't get, even if I want them."

"Come on. Really?" I cocked my head and raised my eyebrow at him. I'd never heard him speak candidly about any of the social shit at Heritage. So why was he doing it now?

"He's right," Bruce said. "That's just how it is right now. How it has always been at school."

"What do you mean?" I asked Bruce. I'd always lumped them together as two tumors in my life that I couldn't cut out. I hadn't stopped to think that they might have their own perspectives on life.

Bruce tapped his pen on the edge of the table. "One thing about school is how people just assume you're one way. Like us. They think we're just rich meatheads. And there's nothing to change that."

"But why would you want to change it?"

"Because it sucks, sometimes," Bruce said after a moment. "And like, with girls, that just means the only girls who want anything to do with either of us," he pointed to himself, and then his brother, "are the airheads."

I grinned. "Like Monica."

"She's a bitch, but she gives it up," Blake said. "Of course, she's nothing like Laine. Laine would never look twice at guys like us. Just Evan."

"I wish it wasn't like that," I muttered before I could stop myself.

"Oooh," Blake said, closing his notebook. "I knew it. You totally thought you had a chance with her."

"No I didn't."

"Somebody really should put Laine in her place," Blake muttered. I didn't try to hide the glare I shot him.

"It'll be better for you once you realize she wants nothing to do with someone like you," Bruce added. "She's a Disney Princess. And you're a frog."

"Thanks for reminding me."

"Look, there's just no other way to really say it." Bruce replied. "We've all been in school together, ever since we were in kindergarten. Twelve years in the Robert Hill Independent School system. You should know this right now."

Blake nodded, and pushed his chair back from the table with a loud scrape.

I motioned to the textbook. "You're not done, Blake. You've still got all those worksheets to fill out."

He sighed. "Can't we just pay you to do it?"

"Like the chores?"

"Sure. Like the chores, you asshole."

"Nope. Only your father pays me." I grinned from the satisfaction of saying that. I might not have had much hold over them, but when it came to being smarter, I always won.

MONDAY, APRIL 15TH

IT RAINED FOR the first two weeks in April; a cold, continuous, dull system wrapped itself around Greater Cincinnati and hung on to everything. No designer rain boots or all-weather jackets could shut out the spring dreariness, and the lack of sunlight added to what, by then, had become a decent depression. Getting out of bed took more effort than brain surgery. Studying for classes and keeping up with assignments required more focus than I wanted to expend, and at dinner a few times my mother accused me of having a bad case of senioritis.

"You're not yourself," she said in early April, over a

plate of burned roast chicken and limp green beans.

"Sure I am," I dismissed her. "It's just that high school is too easy."

Better to lie than tell her the truth. And the truth was, I'd given up any pretense of trying to be happy in this hellhole. I started wearing all black. The fake smile I often wore as a shield against the teasing and taunts of my peers had disappeared from my face. And, as I walked the halls, I glared at all the underclassmen. By the middle of the month, it was working pretty well.

Geoff Megadeth had finally appeared.

"Dude, you're a fucking nightmare to those freshmen." Josh poked me with his shoulder after my latest glare scared away a fat girl with a lacrosse hoodie. She had given me one of those looks that said she'd never glance my way again. *Just what I wanted.*

I looked at him sideways as I turned and shut my locker. "That's the idea."

He sighed when the warning bell rang for first period. From there, we had four minutes to scamper to class before being late. "Let's go. Can't wait to hear what school has waiting for us today. The more you know—"

My snicker interrupted him, and I slammed my locker closed. "Whatever. I just like fucking with them."

I fell into step next to him, and we walked down the long hallway to our first class. Around us the crowd thinned, as students entered classrooms to start another week of learning geometric equations, Spanish verbs and chemistry terms. I didn't make eye contact with anyone, preferring to keep my head down. Less than four weeks to go, and summer would be here. I could make it.

Couldn't I?

"Oh shit," Josh said under his breath as we rounded the corner that linked the main hallway with two others. Heritage High was nothing if not a mix of spidery hallways that wrapped through the Gothic architecture. I looked up in time to regret right away that we'd taken this route. About fifteen students remained in what had been a hallway of dozens five minutes ago.

Laine and Evan were two of those fifteen.

He had her up against the locker, one arm pressed against the metal just above her shoulder, body language that told everyone she was his. Her backpack and lightweight tan jacket lay in a large pile by her feet, which she'd encased in a pair of high-heeled tan rubber boots. One of her legs pressed perpendicularly against the locker, too, and that made her black cotton dress ride up her thighs.

The two of them might have been an ad for a designer perfume.

Even worse, we had no other way to get to our first class. We had to walk right by them, even though all I wanted to do was disappear. *Christ.* Why did I keep on having this kind of horrible luck?

"We'll just keep walking," I told Josh when I saw his eyes widen and his mouth drop open. "Like, it's nothing. No big deal."

"You sure?"

"Do we have any other choice?"

Evan kissed Laine a few times on the neck, the type of typical public display of affection he always favored when it came to her. I never saw them go so far as to make out in the hall, but as a couple they always did just enough to let everyone know they were together. As he kissed her,

her eyes closed, and she rolled her head back against the metal of the locker. I couldn't read her mind, but something about Laine's expression told me she enjoyed this. As I realized that, a few pieces of my heart broke off and faded away for good.

She would never do something like that with me.

"Come on." Josh tugged on my arm, and I noticed that I'd stopped walking in the middle of the hallway. "Class."

"Right." I cleared my throat, and pulled my gaze away from Evan and Laine. "Class."

"Just a few more weeks," Josh replied as he pulled me into the classroom for first period. "A few more weeks and you can forget about her forever."

MONDAY, APRIL 29TH

BIG EVENTS ON the calendar never passed without some sort of tradition at Heritage, and prom was no exception. Tension and excitement about the biggest dance of the year accelerated the week before it, and it started with the fifteen juniors and seniors on prom committee. They charged around school selling tickets, each of them hoping to win a free limo ride to the dance by selling the most. They also wore something "prom-themed" each day of the week leading up to the dance. On Monday it was custom T-shirts, Tuesday it was tuxedo tees. On Wednesday they donned boutonnieres and corsages, Thursday brought out the faux prom court crowns, and Friday, they donned co-ordinated blue, green, and black outfits, the colors of this year's dance.

I had to give them credit for enthusiasm, since most of the outfits looked hideous.

As was also tradition, a voice came over the loudspeaker Monday afternoon during sixth period, about fifteen minutes before the final school bell rang for the day. I couldn't tell who the voice belonged to because of the muffled sound system, but that didn't matter because I already knew just what that person wanted to announce. We all did.

"I have here . . . the nominations for . . . Heritage High Prom Court!" the voice said. All around me students tittered, gasped, and rumbled with excitement. "Six names —three boys, and three girls—are on this year's list."

I gave Mark a knowing look. These names didn't even have to be announced, and the voting had no point whatsoever. Everyone knew who would win this competition. They might as well just crown Laine and Evan now.

"Monica Hargrove. Jillian James, and Laine Phillips! Ladies and gentleman, your nominations for Prom Queen."

Since my classmates broke out into a loud round of applause around me, I joined in, too, with a slow clap. I didn't want to give too much of my energy to something so ridiculous.

"She'll win," Mark said to me, under his breath. "Laine always wins everything."

I didn't reply, because I didn't need to at all. Why argue with the facts?

"Vince Freeman, Neil Harris, Evan Carpenter! I give you the nominations for Prom King."

I rolled my eyes as I heard the cries of excitement from the rest of my classmates. Didn't they expect this?

Didn't they know Evan, Laine, Jillian and the rest of them were all going to be named as the Prom Court? Wasn't this just a script?

"Evan will win," I told Mark. "He's already won."

"You're probably right," Mark replied. He hesitated. "Are you upset that she's taking Evan to prom?"

"Who?"

He gave me a friendly punch on the shoulder. "Come on, man."

I feigned indifference. "What? You thought I'd be upset about Laine? Why would I be upset?"

"Well, since she got back together with him . . . and you like her so much . . ."

"I don't care about that anymore," I lied. "She's going with Evan. Just like she should."

He frowned, and started chewing on the end of his pen. "I don't think they're that happy."

"Sure looked happy to me the other day at his locker. And she's always hanging off him."

"You know how people are sometimes. They just act okay when they're really not." Mark shook his head. "Something about her eyes." I rolled my own, and he changed his tactic. "Are you going to the prom anyway?"

I shrugged. "Hadn't really thought about it," I lied again.

Chapter ten

WEDNESDAY, MAY 1

JOSH ASKED ALLISON to prom after school, in the hallway in front of his locker. By then we all knew they'd go to the dance together anyway, so the whole thing was just a formality. I still felt a twinge of jealousy when he made a big production out of asking her at this end of this stupid song and dance routine he'd made up in the bathroom earlier in the week.

Why did Josh get to have a girlfriend and I didn't?

"Of course I'll go with you," Allison said. Then she kissed Josh in front of me, Nathan, Mark, and a few other kids who hadn't rushed out of school after the last bell rang. She seemed to make him really happy, and they reminded me of one of those paintings about opposites—the artsy girl in dark vintage clothes kissing a nervous guy who liked to wear polo shirts and dark jeans. Kinda cute when you thought about it.

Good thing I had taken to hiding all my emotions under dark clothing and a permanent scowl.

"Are you guys going, too?" Allison asked once she broke the kiss, and we headed to the front door of the school.

"Um, yeah," Nathan muttered, as if this was the first time he'd ever thought about it.

"Sure," Mark said. "I mean, it's prom."

"I'm not going," I said. I pushed open Heritage's glass front door, squinting as the light from the afternoon sun hit my face. "No reason to."

"Come on dude." Josh linked his hand with Allison's. "You have to go."

"No I don't," I replied. I didn't want to talk about this. I wanted to go, but I wasn't going to. No way. Laine would be at prom with that asshole Evan, and all it would do is shove the fact that I would never be with her in my face. I didn't need that kind of torture. I might have been a lot of things, but I wasn't a masochist.

"But prom is the biggest night of the year," Allison replied, sarcastic. "You have to go, Geoff."

"No, I don't." I shifted my backpack from one shoulder to the other as I thought about all the things I could do instead of going to prom, like study for the upcoming AP tests, go see a movie, or play Candy Crush. Yeah. I could find plenty of things to do. I didn't need some idiotic dance to fill up my time.

Allison knocked me on the arm with her free hand. "Come on, it's not like getting dressed up and going to the dance is the worst thing you could do on a Saturday night.

"Why? So I can see her—with someone else?"

Allison stopped walking, and regarded me. "Wow. You really do care about Laine, don't you? It's not a rumor."

I rolled my eyes. "I'm sure you heard plenty."

"Well, of course I did." She hesitated. "Everyone has, I mean. People like to speculate."

"You mean they like to talk."

"Whatever, Geoff." She gave me a half-smile. "It's kinda cute that you like her so much. Very sweet."

I nodded in Josh's direction. "Who would have ever thought Allison was a softie?"

"Of course she is." He threw his arm around her. "And you have to go. You have to. It won't be the same if you don't."

"Maybe." I shrugged. "I thought maybe I might stay home and work on my *World of Warcraft* score."

Everyone laughed, except me. Once the words escaped me mouth, I heard how pathetic I sounded. Jesus Christ. I needed to get over Laine Phillips and accept the fact that she and I would never be together. The sooner I did that, the sooner life would get back to normal, and I could go back to dreaming about the day I would leave Robert "Suburban Hell" Hill.

And that's when my life would start for real

FRIDAY, MAY 3RD

NATHAN HAD A weird look on his face when I walked up to my locker before first period. He stared at me with the same intensity someone would give a beloved science project. I knew him well enough to know just what he was thinking.

"I told you guys. I'm not going to prom." I dropped my book bag on the floor and opened up my locker. My whole academic life stared at me from its insides: thick binders, science texts, planners, and well-worn notebooks, waiting for me to cart them off to another meaningless class. It made me want to roll my eyes, slam the door shut, and walk out of school.

"Come on. You have to go."

"Why does everyone keep saying that?"

"You know Laine's going to win Prom Queen." Nathan leaned up against the locker beside mine, crossed his arms, and studied me. "Huge night for her. Don't you want to see that?"

Sure I did. No doubt. Even if she had rejected me, I still wanted to see her get every award and accolade she deserved. Laine was a beautiful person, inside and out. Of course I wanted to see her win Prom Queen. Prom would be one of the greatest nights of high school for her, even though it would also be a horrible night of hell for me.

"Whatever," I said. "It doesn't matter at all."

"What doesn't matter?"

Laine's voice, which came from somewhere behind me, made me jump. When I turned around she stood there, smiling at me with that infectious, model-esque grin of hers. She looked perfect in pair of dark jeans, simple white T-shirt and scarf. Not that she ever looked less than.

"Hey, Geoff," she said, adding a half-smile once she said my name. Nathan gave me a knowing look, and signaled that he'd see me later before disappearing down the hallway.

"Laine. Hey. Good to see you." I cleared my throat. "So. Are you, um . . . are you excited about prom?"

She raised her eyebrow. "Should I be?"

"Oh, whatever. You know you're going to win this. I mean, everyone loves you . . . Prom Queen is in the bag," I stuttered. Jesus Christ. I was sounding like some kind of idiot. I might as well just drool over her and then start masturbating. Fuck me.

No, fuck everything.

"Nothing in life is guaranteed, Geoff," she said skeptically.

"You're just saying that."

"No, I'm not." She pouted. "I mean it. I'm not betting on anything."

If I'd been in the wrong mood, her constant chipper nature and sunny-side personality would have really gotten underneath my skin. As it was, though, I tolerated it. Scratch that. Maybe I even liked it a little. It certainly kept me interested.

"You'll win," I told her. "You always do."

She rocked back and forth on her heels. "So, um. Are you going to prom?"

"Probably not."

"That's a shame." She glanced down at the floor, and I wondered if she was embarrassed. "I was kinda hoping you would. Just so . . . well . . ." She broke off her sentence, and her eyes widened as something over my shoulder caught her eye. I turned and saw Evan halfway down the hallway. He slammed shut a locker with one hand and started walking toward us, his big body parting the cliques of other students gathered together in the hallway. Evan didn't look at any of them. He just kept his eyes on the two of us.

"Shit," Laine said. "I should . . . anyway . . . um . . ."

She backed away from me, her head still turned. The natural rosiness of her cheeks faded away and the skin around her eyes tightened. Whatever was wrong with her, it had to be pretty bad, because I had never seen that kind of tense body language from her before. Frantic to figure out what to do, my attention flicked back and forth between her and Evan. As he got closer, I saw more of his expression. A scowl danced across his face, and he lumbered down the hallway like a disgusted Paul Bunyan.

"I gotta go, Geoff," Laine said, but just as the words came out of her mouth, Evan made a sharp turn into one of the classrooms about twenty feet away from us. He stared at us as he did it, a deep, menacing frown projecting his annoyance, until he disappeared behind the classroom door.

Laine exhaled, and the large heave of her chest startled me. "Wait, are you okay?"

"Yeah, I guess. I don't know, maybe." Some of the color in her face returned. "Yeah, I'm fine."

"Are you sure?"

She laughed, but it sounded forced. "I'll probably pay for this later."

"Pay for what?"

"Oh, nothing. It's nothing." She pulled back her shoulders, and shook her head. "Just forget I said that."

"Why would you want me to forget it?"

"Geoff, it's nothing." The way she said my name told me to stop asking questions. "Just—I just hope you'll come to prom. That's all I wanted to say."

"Really?" I still couldn't let go of the way I'd just seen Evan look at her. Like he owned her. Like he expected something from her. Like he expected something from me.

"I mean it, Geoff. I wish you would come." She grinned at me, and some of the old Laine had returned. "Come on. If nothing else, well, it's prom. The last school dance we'll ever go to."

"Well, I don't know—"

"Just think about it." She smiled at me, not only with her mouth, but with her eyes. Goddamn it, why did she have to be so darn cute?

The bell rang, saving me. I didn't have to make a decision about prom right then.

In the end, Josh convinced me. More than that, he bought my ticket to prom. After school he stopped at the at the booth the Prom Committee set up next to the auditorium, but I didn't think anything of it because I knew he had a date with Allison. When he whirled around with a conspiratorial grin on his face, though, I knew.

That loyal bastard.

"Prom is on," he said, as he walked up to where I waited for him next to the stairs. "Get ready for a night you will never forget."

"You mean, a night *you* will never forget," I said, making my way down the first few steps and hoping that I read my friend's expression wrong. "Your night with Allison."

"No way." He waved a stack of tickets in my face. "I've got three tickets here. Me. Allison. And you."

"Come on. You know I'm not going. I already told

you and Allison."

"Yeah, you are. You're coming." He handed a ticket over to me, but I didn't take it. It disgusted me. It might as well have been covered in mucus. "You don't even have to pay me back, Geoff."

We stood outside the building now, and all around us students rushed to get in their cars and head home, or to practice. Electricity hung in the air, too, through hushed chatters, girls shooting their prom dates shy glances, and conversations that focused on flowers, dress colors, and tuxedo sizes. This wasn't just any weekend. This was the start of prom weekend. The best weekend in all of our shared high school experiences.

Or so they all said.

"Everyone's going," Josh said, after a couple of seconds of just staring at me like I had a disease. "Everyone."

"Well, not me." I thought about Blake and Bruce. They had dates, of course, two sophomore cheerleaders that hung around their lockers laughing too loud, and who seemed to like the twins for their status on the state championship football team. In fact, I suspected those girls just spent time with my stepbrothers so they could get to the dance themselves. Underclassmen girls were always pulling shit like that. It was something of a status symbol to date a guy two years older, and even more of a triumph to show up at prom.

Not that Blake and Bruce cared if those chicks wanted to use them. They seemed to like having two younger girls follow them around, as if they were Greek gods. Every night at dinner this week they'd been talking about prom, and all week I had wanted to be sick at dinner.

Those fuckers always got everything they wanted. *Everything.*

"Come on man, school dances are overrated," I said, trying to sound like I didn't care and wondering why no one would accept this answer from me. I didn't want to go. No big deal. Why couldn't anyone understand that?

"Whatever, Geoff. If you don't go, Evan wins."

I squinted at my best friend. "What makes you say that?"

"He gets the girl, for sure. He spends the whole night with her, and you won't even see 'er. You'll just be home alone, like some sack, while everyone else in our class has the time of their lives and gets laid."

"Like you and Allison, right?"

"Yeah, like me and Allison." He turned a little bit defensive as he shoved the ticket into my hand. "At least I'm going to get a shot at it. Besides, plenty of people go to prom alone.'"

"No they don't."

"There won't be another prom, Geoff."

I chuckled. "Now you sound like my mother." She'd been trying to get me to go to the dance, too. She worried I'd miss out, and regret it forever. I kept telling her that only idiots worried about stuff like that, but she didn't believe me for even half a second.

He had a point.

Plus, I had a tuxedo already. I got it for Mom's wedding to David, and it still fit. I even had two ties, and one of them might work.

"Okay," I said, still somewhat reluctant. This dance could go either way. "I'll go, but not because I want to. Just for you, Josh."

He laughed and gave me one of those knowing looks. Something told me that he wanted me there for his own entertainment. Oh well. I was going to the biggest dance of the year by myself. What the fuck could go wrong?

Chapter eleven

SATURDAY, MAY 4TH

"YOU LOOK REALLY nice," Mom said from the top of the stairs. "My baby, all grown up. So handsome."

"Thanks." I adjusted my tuxedo and wrinkled my nose as I looked at myself in the mirror. Wearing the tuxedo reminded me too much of the day my mom married David—a day I wanted to forget.

"The jacket fits better now than it used to," she said. "Must be all those workouts you've been doing up here."

I laughed, and smoothed the jacket.

"You're not wearing all black either."

"So you did notice?"

"Of course I noticed. I'm your mother. And I think it's wonderful that you decided to go to prom, and not miss it." Mom had a gleam in her eye, like this whole moment made her sentimental, or even a little bit sad. Since Dad died, I'd seen that look on her face a few too many times, and I hated it so much.

"Are Blake and Bruce still here?" I turned my attention to the pile of clothes on my bed. My car keys were in there, somewhere, along with my solo ticket to the prom. At least I knew Mark, Josh, Allison and Nathan would be there. Dread welled up inside me, despite the fact that I kept telling myself Prom couldn't be too bad, even if I didn't have Laine as my date.

"The twins just left." She nodded at my bed. "Mind if I sit down?"

"Sure."

Even after she sat, she kept her body rigid, as if she had something on her mind and she didn't know how to begin talking about it. Her eyes followed me as I shook out my tuxedo jacket and put my car keys in my pants pocket.

"I still can't believe you are so old now. Senior Prom. And graduation around the corner."

I rolled my eyes. "Yeah. Can't wait for that."

She watched me adjust my tie two more times. "Geoff, do you like the life we have now?"

I frowned, but didn't look up as the thought crossed my mind that this might be a trick question. Better to be as diplomatic as possible. "It's great. You seem happy."

"That's not what I meant. I'm not talking about myself. I mean, for you. Do you like our life?" She broke off and took a deep breath. "Of course, I probably don't have to ask that. I know you hate David."

Mom put her hand on my arm and forced me to look at her. "You might not like him, but he likes you. He knows you're headed for something bigger than this. Something bigger than Robert Hill." She sighed. "He wants the same thing for the twins, but he doesn't think they'll get there. But he knows you will."

I gawked at her, confused. "He doesn't talk to me, except to tell me whatever chores he wants me to do, and when he wants something from me, like tutoring Blake and Bruce. I don't even think he knows my middle name."

Mom tilted her head at me and narrowed her eyes.. "Come on, Geoff. Don't be so dramatic like that. He knows your full name is Geoffrey Paul Miller."

"Whatever. I can't deal with this right now." I picked up my jacket from the bed. "It's almost six forty-five. Dance starts at seven. I should probably go."

"Are you mad at me?" She stood up from the bed. "Do you wish I hadn't married David?"

"No," I lied. Then I pulled on my jacket and grabbed my keys.

"Listen, I know I haven't been the best mother. I'm sorry."

A large sigh escaped my lungs. "You don't have to be sorry, Mom. It's fine. I know things were tough when Dad died. I know that. You did the best you could."

"You know, you really do look handsome." She paused as if considering something. "Why don't you take my BMW?"

"What?"

"The BMW." She blinked at me a few times. "Do you want to drive it to the dance?"

"Really?" I didn't even try to hide my excitement.

"Sure. Why not?"

"But what if I crash it?"

"I know you won't do that, honey." She motioned for me to follow her down to the garage. Once we got there, she handed me the keys to her black 2012 528i sedan, a fiftieth birthday gift from David. She never let anyone drive the thing, so I didn't know how to respond as I took the keys. David had professionals wash and wax this car once a week and the sedan had an all leather interior, as well as every option BMW offered. Just riding in it made a person feel rich, and now she wanted me to drive it.

"Like I said, I know you won't do anything stupid," Mom said when she saw my hesitation. "I know the son I raised."

"Well . . ." I laughed. "You know, I was thinking later about getting drunk—"

"You better be trying to be funny."

"Yep. I wouldn't get do something stupid like that." I smiled as I hugged her small body. She felt so fragile and delicate in my arms, as if I might break her by squeezing too tight. "This is really nice of you. Really nice. No, better than that. Pretty awesome."

When I pulled away from the hug, she had a huge grin on her face, too. "Get in. It's prom night. And it's a special night."

I unlocked the door and sank into the soft leather driver seat. The car still smelled new, even thought she'd owned it for about year, and as I inhaled, a change came over me. Was it confidence? Swagger? I couldn't tell for sure, but even when I tried to shake it off, the feeling didn't go away. After a moment, I let it register that I was going to drive this car, this amazing car—even if I wouldn't be driving the sedan to Laine's house to pick her up, or to any other hot girl's house as a consolation. At least it would be a fun ride down to The Syndicate.

"Just do me a favor," Mom said, after I clicked the seatbelt in place.

"What?"

"Try to give David a chance," she said. "He's not that bad." When I sighed, she leaned over and dusted the shoulder of my tuxedo jacket. "People aren't so horrible if you just let them show you who they are, honey."

Mom shut the car door and waved as she punched the button to open the garage door. I waved back, turned the car on, threw it in reverse, and pulled out of the garage. The engine hummed and responded in a way I'd never felt in any other car. No wonder David and Mom treated this car like a piece of fine art. Even the sound system made music crisper and clearer—at least, to my ears.

When I glanced in the rear-view mirror about halfway through the drive, I smiled at myself. Might as well try to have fun, since it was Prom night, after all.

"Can I check you in, Geoff?" asked Ms. Knight, the tenth grade algebra teacher, and a prom chaperone. She smiled up at me from a wide wooden table where she sat next to Mr. Langston. She wore a blue taffeta dress with a beige crochet shrug that highlighted the 100 pounds she needed to lose. He wore an ill-fitting brown suit with a blood-red tie and mustard stain on the collar of his shirt. What a pair.

"Sure," I said, taking a prom packet from the table. A brochure listed the dinner menu, small silent auction, and raffle that the Heritage Boosters set up near the dance floor. My eyebrow arched when I realized someone at the prom that night would win a 60-inch flat screen TV at the after prom party.

"Don't forget to hand in your vote for King and Queen," said Mr. Langston. "It's in the back of the packet."

"Okay."

"Voting ends at nine p.m."

"Let me just hand you my vote now." A shuffle of the papers showed me the ballot. The names for King and Queen danced and mocked me on the page. Picking Prom Queen was easy, but choosing a king was hard. So I left that space blank.

"No date tonight?"

I looked up from the Prom Court list. "Nope."

"Lots of people go to proms alone," said Ms. Knight, and her voice made it obvious she wanted to sound kind and disarming.

"Sure they do," I replied as I handed in my vote.

"Thanks for voting, I see you're at the table with your friends. Table fifty-six." She motioned for me to give her my wrist, which she then fastened a light blue wristband around. "Most of them are already here."

"Great."

I nodded at them both, then walked past the table and down about five stairs. Large round tables of eight surrounded a rectangular dance floor in front of the stage. Long strands of white lights and sparkling stars hung down from the ceiling, no doubt part of the "Prom In the Stars" theme. The decor added to the busy theme of the event space, which was meant to be a throwback to gangsters, Prohibition, art deco and the 1930s. Waiters in red jackets with overstuffed trays dropped off plates of salad to the waiting junior and senior class.

Table fifty-six sat in the middle of the room, near the

back. Josh, Mark and Nathan already sat at the table with their dates. Mark and Nathan had each brought sophomore girls from marching band, but I didn't know their names. Josh sat next to Allison Nichols, of course. She'd exchanged her black lipstick for a blood red one, and her combat boots for a gray dress with black lace around the hem. In truth, she looked pretty and happy. But I guess prom did that to people.

"Great to see you, Geoff," Josh said, and I wondered if I saw a triumphant gleam in his eye. He stood up and clapped me on the back once I reached the table.

"Yeah, you too." Despite my misery, I meant it, so I added a smile as I took my seat next to Josh, and tried to ignore the empty one next to me that sat as a constant reminder of the date I had never asked to join me. Not that it mattered. Laine already had a date—Evan—everyone knew it, and that information played over and over and over again in my head, as if it wanted to taunt me. Even worse, when I looked up from my wilted salad covered in ranch dressing, I noticed I had a direct line of sight to her table.

Damn it.

Josh tossed me a look that I caught in my peripheral vision, and right away I knew he'd seen her, too. Across the room, Laine threw her head back and laughed at something Jillian had said in her ear. There she went again, always laughing. Always smiling. Always out of reach, this time with her hair piled on top of her head, and a glittering crystal tucked into the hairstyle. She also wore a large rhinestone necklace and a black strapless dress. I couldn't tell if it was long or short. It didn't really matter.

"Man," Josh muttered. "You really do have it so bad

for her."

"We've already established that." I turned back to the salad and stabbed a cherry tomato with my fork.

"Like I've said before. Girls like that don't go for guys like us. Ever. It's not in their DNA."

"Real optimistic, bro."

"Just don't want you to get hurt. Again."

I looked up from the salad and shot him a withering look. "She's not going to hurt me. Again."

"She's taken. That's all."

"Who's taken?" asked Allison, a piece of dinner roll poised to enter her mouth.

"No one," I told her. "No one at all."

Allison gave me one of those looks that made me think she knew who I was talking about anyway.

"Would you like your entree?" asked a waitress who stood next to my left. I jumped at her voice; I hadn't even noticed she stood there.

"Uh, sure," I said.

She sat down a plate of chicken masala on a bed of risotto.

"Mm, chicken," I said. "Looks delicious."

"Almost as delicious as Laine," Josh replied. I kicked him under the table, and he choked on his food. "I mean, as delicious as you, Allison."

She sniffed. "Whatever."

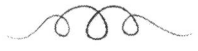

Ms. Knight took the stage an hour later as the waiters passed around chocolate cake desserts with raspberry compote drizzle. Someone who didn't know her might have said she looked tipsy, but I knew better. She was the kind of teacher who went around saying things like "I'm high on life," and "Happiness is my high!"

Prom night brought out the best in a woman like her.

"Good evening, junior and senior class." The microphone she spoke into had distorted the sound, so her voice sounded scratchy and far away. The fat rolls spilled out of her dress and threatened to swallow the mic whole, taking it somewhere no one in that room wanted to go. That alone kept my attention. "Are you all having a great night at prom?"

Everyone clapped and answered her with a collective yell.

"Well, I'm glad to hear it! Every one of you looks so adorable in your outfits! Just like little cakes!" She took a few steps across the stage to make sure she addressed everyone. "And things only will get better, because the night has just started! Who's ready to elect your Prom King and Queen?"

Did she really need to ask that question?

Mr. Langston walked up on the stage with a gold envelope, and presented it to her as the room erupted again in a round of applause and hollers from my classmates. In Mr. Langston's other hand he held two crowns, one for a girl, and one for guy. He leaned into the microphone, just a few inches from Ms. Knight's breasts. "The results are in! Are you ready?"

More cheers came from the crowd, and my eyes found Laine's. She smiled at me, and my heart jumped to my throat. Out of my peripheral vision, Mr. Langston lifted up the envelope and opened it with an awkward flourish.

"Your Prom King is . . . drumroll please.... Evan Carpenter!"

Some things about high school were just so predictable. Insert eye roll.

"Why did we even vote?" Josh wondered aloud as the room broke into loud applause.

"Exactly," Allison muttered.

Evan pushed back his chair, and danced his way to the stage, as if he owned the room. His face looked redder than usual, and when he reached Ms. Knight, he kissed her on the cheek with a loud smack. Then he knelt so that Mr. Langston could place the cheap crown on his head.

Allison giggled. "That crown looks so tiny on his huge head."

"It's really bad," I said. "Looks like a crown from Burger King."

"Are you ready to hear who will be Prom Queen?" Ms. Knight asked, once Evan had stepped to the side.

Again, I wondered why the school had even bothered to vote on this. I could have elected the Prom Queen back when we'd all been freshman. Things never changed at Heritage High School. Whoever a person was to their classmates by seventh grade, they were that very same person to their classmates here, on prom night. No one ever broke out of place in the caste system. No one.

"Your Prom Queen is . . ." Ms. Knight opened the envelope, and her eyes widened in mock surprise. "Laine Phillips!"

Laine stood up from her table, as the room erupted into cheers once again. She should have known she would win, but the goofy grin on her face told me that, no matter how much anyone else expected it, she never did. Not for a second. Happiness and surprise radiated from her, and even I clapped as she made her way up the stage to take her place next to Evan. Once she had the silver and rhinestone crown on her head, she reminded me of a frosted Barbie doll.

"She so gorgeous you wish you could hate her, but then she's so nice that you just can't," Allison said, as Evan and Laine posed for photos destined to take a place on the front page of the school newspaper and their own yearbook spread. "Everyone just loves her."

"Yep, they do," Josh replied. "Especially Geoff, here."

I hit him once on the arm with the back of my hand, and shot him a warning look. "Shut up."

Too late. A smug smile floated across Allison's face. "He's still in love with her, just like the rest of the school."

"I'm not in love with her," I protested, my voice rising in urgency. "I'm not in love with her!"

"It's okay." Allison nodded at the stage where Evan and Laine had just started their dance together as King and Queen. "Everyone is. It's just a shame she won't ever stop dating Evan."

Heritage High's PTA, staff, and the parents of students prided themselves on giving the best they could, but that didn't mean a good DJ for the biggest event of the school year. Some things just weren't in the budget. Instead, we danced to an iPod playlist piped through the speakers, but I think I was the only one who noticed. Or who even really cared. Everyone else looked content to pack the rectangular parquet floor, and sweat away in fancy pastel dresses and rented tuxedos.

About an hour into the dancing, most of the girls ditched their shoes, and many of the guys wore patches of sweat on their backs. They yelled comments back and forth to each other and took hundreds of photos on their cell phones for Instagram, Twitter, and Facebook accounts.

"This music sucks," Allison said as "Electric Boogie" began. All around our small group of friends, the crowd spread out to perform the line dance that accompanied the music. A longtime staple of weddings, bar mitzvahs, and school dances, almost everyone at Heritage knew that dance better than they wanted to admit. Funny, how a song like that had so much staying power.

"Come on," Josh said, as he fell in line with the crowd. "A school dance isn't a dance without this song."

"Whatever, I can't stand it," Allison replied. "I'm going to the ladies room." She smiled at both of us and disappeared into the crowd.

"It is kinda . . . well . . ." I said to Josh, but then I broke off, because some commotion diagonal from us on the dance floor caught my eye. In fact, what I saw brought me to a total halt.

Both Evan and Laine had stopped dancing. A deep frown cut canyons on her face, and she narrowed her eyes as she spoke to him. Anyone who saw her would have known she was angry. Evan said a few words to her and swayed a little, still wearing the cheap crown on his head. Unsatisfied, she pulled him off the dance floor through the rows of tables, and over to a dark corner near the banquet hall exit, away from everyone else and behind a large sign with the prom theme painted on it. No one followed them, but that didn't really surprise me. The crush of students and music created chaos on the dance floor, as my classmates snapped photos of each other with their cell phones, danced in large groups, and laughed, as if this was the last night of their lives. They were all having too much fun to notice the argument.

And that argument reignited once Evan and Laine made it behind that poster. From where I stood, I watched them yell, their faces inches from each other. Evan's face turned so red that I wondered if it would turn purple before long. Laine looked like she might cry at any moment. I stared at them until curiosity took over every cell in my body. "I wonder what—"

"What?" Josh yelled over the music "What's wrong?" He stopped his awkward interpretation of the line dance and turned in the direction where I stared. By then, the argument between Laine and Evan looked heated to about five hundred degrees. "Oh. Shit."

"Dude, I wonder if she's okay. He looks pissed."

"So does she." I took one step in their direction, and Josh threw out his arm to stop me, angling his body so I couldn't cut an easy path. "No way. Don't go over there."

"Why can't I? We're friends."

"That's between them." He put his hand on my shoulder, but I still had a good view of Laine and Evan over his arm. She had crossed her arms, and swayed a little. Whatever this was, it was bad. Really bad.

Epic, even.

I threw Josh's arm off my shoulder. "Look, I'm her

friend. We're friends. And you know, Evan's an asshole. I'm going over there to see if she's okay."

"Really I don't think you should—"

"You can't stop me!"

"Come on, Geoff."

I silenced him with a glare and made my way through the crowd of sweaty juniors and seniors. With each step, the argument intensified. Evan threw up his hands a few times. Laine covered her face in disgust. She backed away from him. He followed her. She said something to him and I saw him clench his right fist. The fact that my classmates ignored it all pissed me off. Couldn't they take a break from their self-absorbed lives and notice what was happening right in front of them? Not even the chaperones stepped in, too busy dancing with the students. Why was I the only one seeing this? Why was I the only one who cared?

What the hell was wrong with people? Prom might have been fun, but that didn't give them an excuse to act like their stupid lives were the only thing that mattered. Did it? And then, just as I made it to the tables, the unthinkable happened.

Evan slapped Laine.

He reached his broad hand back, said something I couldn't hear, waited for her response, and cracked her once across the cheek. Just once, but one slap was enough for me. My own anger crashed around in my body as I took the fastest strides I could to reach them. Prom faded into the background, and I blocked out everything else but that moment. No way was he going to slap her and get away with it. I didn't care who he was, or about the crown he'd just won. Evan shouldn't treat Laine like trash, or like she was less than worthy to be around him. No one should. No one.

Laine yelled at him, holding her cheek. He swayed again as he replied, and even I saw the unnatural heaviness in in his lids. She shoved him away from her, and then did something that made me want to kiss her even more. She walked away.

No, she fled.

Laine walked over to her table and grabbed her purse just seconds before I made it over to them. Her clouded face didn't meet anyone's eye, so I couldn't tell if she noticed me. All I knew was that I was the only one at prom who'd even witnessed that slap. I was the only other person in the room who knew Evan really was a certified asshole.

With one eye on her, and the other on Evan, I considered my options. I could go over there, hit him, and defend her. I probably wouldn't win, but the moment would be one to savor. Or I could go after her, see if she was okay, and seize the opportunity to be alone with the one girl who never failed to make my heart swell.

I sucked in a breath. This really wasn't a decision, at all.

Chapter twelve

LAINE STOOD ALONE on the curb next to the valet stand. She wrapped her arms around her ribs like she was cold, and I knew before I even reached her side that the asshole had made her cry. In fact, once I got to her, I saw it for myself. Mascara ran down her face in four watery streaks, and somewhere along the line she had smudged her red lipstick. Her black dress suddenly looked too big.

Sad.

For a minute, I wondered if I really should just go back inside prom, find Evan, and punch him until he needed plastic surgery. That asshole could have benefited from someone rearranging his face, and I wouldn't have minded being the one to do it. But then, her words stopped me.

"He's drunk, Geoff. That's all it is," she managed between sniffles. "He's like that when he gets drunk."

"Laine, he slapped you. I saw it." My hand reached out to touch her bare shoulder, but then I stopped myself. "Are you okay?"

"It wasn't hard. Really. It didn't hurt."

"But he hit you!" The way she bit her lip made me

press further. "What is this shit? Has he done it before?"

"No—not—" She broke off, and looked away. "Yes. One other time."

"Just one?" When she didn't answer, I pressed her again. "What about that time I saw that bruise? Did he do that to you?"

"Yes."

"What the fuck, Laine?"

"Well—he sometimes gets angry."

She might not have admitted it, but I had my answer. Evan had hit her before, so many times that he'd made her afraid of him. I exploded in anger. "That's not okay! Jesus Christ. It's not okay. It's a crime!"

When she still didn't look at me, I shut my eyes and cursed myself for not realizing this problem before. Of course Evan would do something unacceptable like this. He'd gotten away with everything else in life. My next words shot out like hot bullets. "Are you kidding me? This is serious. It's not okay."

"I know it's not," she said. "But I don't know what do to about it."

"Oh my God," I said, as I went over in my mind the past conversations I'd had with Laine. "That's why you left that day at the overlook, isn't it? You're afraid of him."

She sniffled. "Maybe. I don't know. I thought we'd get back together and he'd be better, but—he's not. Well, not when he's like this. He's not the same person anymore."

"Have you told anyone?"

"No . . . I mean . . . what am I going to say to them? It would just come back on me. And Evan's invincible."

"No one's invincible."

When my eyes opened, she looked even smaller, even more broken. This was Senior Prom, for fuck's sake. Supposed to be the "best night of our lives." Goddamn that jerkoff. I sighed, put my hand on her shoulder, and turned her body toward me. When she still didn't turn her head, I moved it for her with my right index finger.

"Leave him. Dump him."

A few more tears fell down her face. "I'm planning to do that. After graduation."

"Graduation?"

"That's not long."

"He doesn't love you. He doesn't." I pointed at her cheek. "That's not love, Laine."

"He brought a flask of bourbon. It's in his jacket pocket." She peered down at her shoes. Her chest heaved from a deep breath. "He says it takes a lot of liquor before he gets a buzz, because he's so big."

"I can't believe this is happening." I shook my head. "He's a really bad person."

"He used to love me. I know that."

"Love? Come on."

"He did this summer, before school started, but this hasn't been that great of a senior year for him. He's different. His parents are going through a horrible divorce, and he's going to have to pay for whatever his scholarship won't cover at Ohio State—all his food, and everything. He's pretty much on his own." She sighed. "It changed him a lot. He's not the person I used to know."

"You're making excuses for him!"

"I'm not. I'm just—I don't want anyone to know because they won't understand. People don't get it. They don't get me."

"You left that day because you didn't want to make him mad," I said. "Jesus. What an asshole."

"Well, I learned pretty quickly that it was just easier to go with the flow, to keep him happy," she said as her eyes fell to the ground. "I thought I could just make it through the next couple of weeks, and then it would be easier because high school would be over."

"He doesn't know what he has with you. He doesn't." When she shivered, I took off my tuxedo jacket and wrapped it around her shoulders. She accepted it without protest. "It's stupid if you stay with him any longer. Really stupid."

I still felt angry. No, furious. Livid. Pissed beyond belief. Why hadn't I been more observant? Why hadn't her friends? How long had things been like this?

"You don't understand. It's complicated. He's only like that when he's drunk. The rest of the time, he's fine."

"Do you know what you're saying? You sound like some kind of cliché." I cleared my throat, as I struggled to say something that sounded right. "You could be some kind of after school special. We all could—this whole stupid school, this place . . ."

Her wide eyes finally met mine. "No, please. You can't—please don't tell anyone. This . . . I don't want . . ."

"I should go back in there and kick his ass." My eyes darted over to the glass door entrance to The Syndicate. "I'm sure I could get a few good punches in before he breaks my neck."

She laughed, and when I saw her smile again the tension in my back faded away a little.

"I want to leave," she said after a moment. Then she

opened up her small beaded purse, and started digging around for something. "Like, right now. It's just easier that way. I really want to get away from here."

"You don't want to go to that lame after prom? Someone's going to win a huge ass TV." I looked at my watch. 11:15 p.m. After prom started at the high school in forty-five minutes. "We could go. Or you could go with your friends."

"I don't want to go," she whispered. "I don't care about it anymore."

"Yeah. Me neither."

I sucked in my breath, and took another step to her. The crisp night air seemed to change as I did, and I wondered if this was my moment: my one perfect moment. The moment I had waited over a year for, maybe for all of high school—the moment that toyed with my mind every time I saw her update her status on social media. After another long breath, I decided it was.

Her lips tasted like cherry bubble gum lip-gloss, and she didn't protest as mine kissed them. At first it was just a peck, a small brush. Then I grew bolder, and my lips lingered on hers a little longer. Then a little bit more. Then my tongue entwined with hers as I reached out and slid my hand around her warm neck. These were kisses I wanted to remember forever. These were kisses I had fantasized about. And these were kisses I needed to last indefinitely.

They almost did, but Laine pulled away after a few moments.

"What took you so long?"

"So long?" I murmured.

"You could have done this months ago." She smiled into my mouth. "Maybe I wish you had."

I swayed for a second, shocked.

"What about that day back in March, Geoff, when we were in the car? Why didn't you?"

"You were dating Evan." I frowned. "He was your boyfriend. I wasn't going to mess with that."

She sighed. "I know. But I wish...I just wish you'd acted on it." A small smile tugged at her lips. "Or maybe I should have. Didn't you want me to?" She pulled me a little closer. "You wanted me to."

"Wow, Miss Confident." My hands traveled down her back, and I shivered. I loved holding her. She was like something forbidden that only I could have. Oh God, I wanted her so much.

"Confidence will get you everywhere," she said after a moment.

"I'm starting to find that out," I whispered.

Laine grabbed hold of the buttons on my tuxedo shirt and bit her lip. "You wanted to, right?

"Now you don't sound so sure of yourself."

She grinned. "Well, I'm just checking."

"Of course I did." My arm snaked around her waist. Maybe that would steady me. Or maybe it just felt like heaven. Now if only I could keep my eyes from darting from her mouth to her breasts. Oh God, those breasts . . .

"I honestly never thought you would." She placed a few kisses on my neck, close to my ear. "I thought maybe you were too scared because of Evan, or that you didn't like me like that."

"I'm glad we've got that out of the way." I kissed her lips once more.

"Listen," she said, sounding a little breathless. She linked her hand with mine. "I don't want to go to the after prom. But I don't want to go home, either. I can't go home."

"Can't?"

"Not like this. I'm a total mess." She shuddered. "And I don't want my parents asking questions about Evan. They will. Trust me."

"Where do you want to go?" I would have taken Laine anywhere she wanted, even if it meant driving all night, booking an airplane ticket, or finding a magic carpet.

"I've been thinking." She arched her perfect left brow. "Some place fun that's open late."

"The bowling alley? I think they close at two."

"No, silly. Not there." She fished around in her purse again, and then pulled out two small, blank plastic cards. "I noticed I had these a few moments ago. Evan's an idiot."

I frowned, not following her.

"He got us a hotel room at The Cincinnatian," she added. "Or, maybe his brother got it for us, I'm not sure. Anyway, we were supposed to go there after we went to After Prom for about an hour."

"Whoa. The Cincinnatian's expensive."

"Evan thought if he took me to a fancy hotel that I'd forgive him for the way he's been treating me." She snickered, but I heard the disgust behind it. "The room has a Jacuzzi, though."

"I don't have my swimsuit."

"Maybe you won't need it," she breathed, then stepped closer to me, and one slim leg pressed against mine. "What I'm saying, silly, is that I want to go there with you."

I gulped. "You do?"

What did she mean by this? Was she saying she wanted to have sex? With me? Oh God, I hoped she was. I wouldn't turn her down. Not Laine Phillips. Not after those kisses. Not on prom night.

No way.

"Sure." She squeezed my hand. "We can order room service and charge it to their credit card. Revenge."

"Sounds like a plan," I said, still hardly daring to believe this was happening. "I'll get the car."

I drove the BMW like a crazed meth head.

The Cincinnatian Hotel was only about a seven-minute drive from The Syndicate, but the car couldn't take us there fast enough. My hand shook on the steering wheel as we hit every single red light during the small trek from Newport to downtown. Laine just laughed and turned up the radio. Justin Timberlake screamed about being high on a pusher love girl. For once I knew what he meant, because Laine, her perfume, and the faint smell of salty grease in her hair made me feel high. She laughed every time we stopped at a light, and I held my breath on the ride until I saw the grand old hotel. Maybe she wouldn't back out of this after all.

With a long sigh, I pulled the car up to the valet stand, got out, and tossed the keys at the barrel-chested old man wearing a red porter's cap and brown jacket with gold buttons. I did my best to wear a stony, suave expression as I opened the passenger door, and ushered Laine into the lobby of the hotel. I didn't want anyone asking what the hell we were doing there, even though I asked myself that about thousand times on the drive over.

I didn't breathe again until the elevator doors closed.

"Nice moves." She laughed. "I've actually never been to this hotel before."

"Me either."

All I knew was that Mom and David came here after their wedding. Gross. Not the mental image I needed to have right then.

Room 203 had a king-sized bed, a large flat screen TV on the wall, a small desk, mini-bar, and love seat. The lights on the nightstands clicked on when the door opened. The room also had the largest bathroom I'd ever seen in a hotel with two sinks, a wide Jacuzzi tub, and a separate shower made of glass.

My breath hitched when she closed the room door behind us. I was standing in a hotel room, all alone with Laine Phillips, and she wanted to be here with a sucker like me. This wasn't happening.

Was it?

A thousand questions rumbled around in my head. Would I wake up any time soon? Would we fuck? Would she want me to make love to her? Did I know how to make love? What if I wasn't any good? What if I came too early? What if she hated the way I looked naked? What the hell was someone like me doing with a girl like her? What if she didn't want sex at all? What if she laughed at me once I took my clothes off?

"So, ugh—what do you want to do?" I staggered around in my head, trying to figure out what to say, and willing my dick to stay in line. I didn't want to get prematurely hard. Well, I sort of didn't, and I sort of did. My fucking hormones danced up and down my spine, and then they dueled in my stomach. I worried I might not be able to keep them in check, either.

She plopped down on the white bedspread, and the puffy crinoline skirt of her dress fanned out around her like a black sunflower. I didn't know if I should sit down next to her, so I picked the love seat that faced her.

"So."

"So," I repeated. "Um. This is a nice room."

She glanced around. "Yeah. It's not bad. Evan has good taste sometimes."

"So, what do you want to do?"

"I think SNL is on," she said. She grabbed the large black remote off the table. "And I think it's a new one." She pressed a button, and the TV flipped on to WLWT, the local NBC station that was just finishing its newscast for the night. She tossed the remote on the bed and kicked of her tan snakeskin shoes. "Gosh, it feels good to get out of those."

"Yeah, they don't look comfortable," I said, hoping I didn't have stinky feet as I slipped off my own black dress shoes.

"Oh this is a new one," she said, as the SNL opening sketch came on the TV. She patted the spot next to her. "Why don't you join me? We can watch it together."

Like anyone would turn that invitation down.

"Okay. Um. Do you want something to drink from the mini bar?"

"Sure. Make it good."

"How good?"

"Surprise me."

I opened up the fridge next to the love seat and found two cold cans of Diet Coke next to a couple of bottles of bourbon and vodka. While the monologue played, I dumped them together into two plastic cups. She laughed every few seconds at something the actors said, and each time I fell in love with her a tiny bit more. By the time the host stepped out on stage to warm up the audience, I wanted to marry her.

Okay, maybe not marry. Maybe get a tattoo with her name in cursive across my ankle. Something permanent, like that. Anything to make sure I would never forget her.

"Ohhhhhh, I love the SNL digital shorts," she said, as I handed her a cup. "I hope they have one tonight."

Laine stretched her legs out on the bed, and leaned her back against the headboard. I mimicked her, and we sat in silence for a while, watching the sketches and laughing, the fan from the air conditioner the only other sound in the room. As we sat there, I tried not to spit out the drink the few times I sipped it. It tasted like cough medicine. I shouldn't have been so liberal with the bourbon.

"You like a strong drink, don't you?" she said, during a commercial for Skyline Chili. "A really strong drink."

"Hey, you said to make it good."

"I know, but that's really—it's really, strong." She set it on the bedside table, and turned to me. "Are you nervous, Geoff?"

"Nervous?"

"We're alone in a hotel room. That would make some people nervous."

"No." I glanced down at my cup, and my hands shook. "Yes."

"Okay. Me too." She leaned over and took the cup

from me, placing it next to hers. "Thanks for rescuing me, by the way."

"I didn't rescue you, Laine."

"Well, you were the only one who checked on me out there." She closed her eyes, and her head fell back against the headboard. "All my friends were there. All of them, and none of them noticed anything. God, some friends, huh?"

"Maybe they did notice," I lied. "Maybe they didn't know what to do."

"Still. Some friends."

I studied her as the lights from the TV fell on her face. It didn't look like Evan's hand had left a mark on her cheek, and only the barest bit of a mascara streak remained near her left eyelid. Even after a hard cry, her puffy face seemed angelic and vulnerable. She was like a broken but beautiful Christmas present, and she was with me. Me. Geoffrey Paul Miller.

Time to man up, and seize the moment.

I leaned in and brushed my lips against the dip underneath her left eye. When she responded, I planted a trail of kisses down her cheek, and to her lips. My lips softly pressed against hers, and I tasted that familiar bubble gum. It had an almost comforting scent, and my hand found its favorite place on the back of her neck, at the base of her up do.

"Don't stop kissing me," she said against my mouth. "You're a good kisser."

I grew bolder with her words. My kisses turned urgent, and my tongue cut a path into her mouth, where it twisted with hers. She held onto my shirt, and before I knew it, I was hard and desperate, but I didn't know what to do about it. She must have sensed it, because she popped a few of the buttons on my shirt before she slid further down on to the bed.

"It's okay, Geoff." She sounded out of breath. "I want this."

"You do?"

I held my head above hers, and our eyes locked. If we were going to stop this, we had to stop it right then. I held my breath for another beat. If she stopped this, it wouldn't be the worst thing that ever happened to me. I might even laugh about it later. When I was fifty. And drunk. After about $50,000 worth of therapy.

Laine reached up and drew her finger down my jaw line, not taking her eyes off mine. "You have a nice jaw. Has anyone ever told you that?"

"Nope."

"You're really kinda handsome.. I like your sandy hair."

"My mom says I got it from my dad."

Her other hand reached up and found the hidden zipper on the side of her dress. I heard the twist of metal as she slid it open, and, in that moment, there couldn't have been a sweeter sound in the world. I knew I should take whatever happened next as slow as I could. I should, I should, I should . . .

"This is happening, isn't it?"

"Yeah," she said. "I'm glad it's happening with you."

I kissed Laine again, and she guided my hand to the opening of the dress. I shivered when my hand touched her side, curving into the flesh beneath her armpit, centimeters from her breast. I kissed her out of sheer terror, scared to death she would notice how fast my heart pounded, and feel the sweat I knew had formed on the back of my neck. I kissed her out of desperation. And I kissed her because I knew nothing after that night would ever be the same.

After a few moments, she resumed unbuttoning my shirt, and when she opened the last one I could take it no longer. Neither could she. We pulled apart from each other so I could slip out of my shirt, and she pulled off her dress, returning to me in a pair of black pasties and black underwear. She popped the button on my pants and I gasped, knowing this was the moment of no return. I reached a tentative hand out and cupped her now free breast, my hand caressing a mix of silicone pasty and warm, tender flesh.

This was better than anything I had ever imagined, all the times I'd looked at Internet porn late at night on the computer. Not just better. Intimate. More subtle. And live.

"Can I take these off?" I asked against her mouth as my hand drew a circle around the pasties.

She nodded, and bucked her hips against me as I pulled them off her nipples. Then she yanked down her underwear and lay naked underneath me, officially the first real woman I had ever seen this way. I paused to take in the sight. She had a flat stomach and small round breasts, and when I ran my hand over her bony hip, she shivered.

"Now you have to get naked, Geoff," she prompted.

Oh, right.

With my eyes still on her, I moved off the bed and unzipped my pants. Then I slid them down my legs, and stood next to the bed in my boxer shorts.

"You're still not naked," she said. "And do you have one?"

My tongue thickened in my mouth. "Have one what?"

"A condom?"

I blinked at her. Condoms? I hadn't thought about this part. I couldn't bring myself to even say the word. God, she made me so nervous. Like any second I might pass out from the combination of adrenaline and hormones that coursed through my body like a flood. I was about to have sex. Right then. With Laine Phillips. Who had time to think about the small stuff?

"Do you have one?" she asked again.

"Well . . . I mean . . ." I struggled with what to say next. "You really have done this before, haven't you?"

"Just with Evan a couple of times," she admitted. "It wasn't good. He was—well, I don't know. Maybe I don't want to talk about it. Does it matter, though?" Her voice turned small and unsure.

"No. Not at all."

It really didn't. I didn't care. She was here with me now. In this bed. Naked. Wanting me. That's what I cared about. Behind me, on the TV, SNL introduced a band I had never heard of as the musical act. I barely heard it. If I could have, I would have stopped time, so that all I had for the rest of my life was this moment with her. It might have been love. It might have been lust. It was probably somewhere in the middle.

I didn't really care what it was.

"Geoff," she said, snapping me out of my thoughts. "Do you have a condom with you?"

"Um." I frowned, and then my stomach twisted. Thank God for Josh Anderson. What a friend. I was about to owe him a million bucks. "Yeah." I dug around my pants until I found my wallet. There, inside the front flap, lay the red-wrapped condom he'd given me a few weeks earlier at lunch. I held it out to her. "I have this one."

"Okay." She grinned at me, satisfied. "I'm ready if you are."

I pulled down my boxer shorts and crawled on top of her. As I did, she found the condom with one hand, and my hardness with her other. I closed my eyes. Everything seemed to crash over me at once—all the time I had waited, my feelings for her, the bizarreness of that night, and now the intimacy of this moment.

"I'll be fine," she said. "Don't worry about hurting me."

"Hurting you?" My eyes flew open. I wanted to do plenty of things to her, but I didn't want to hurt her. "I don't want to hurt you."

She giggled against my chest. "You're pretty big."

"I am?"

"You won't hurt me," she said against my mouth. "So don't worry." She kissed me again, and I responded, my hands somewhere in her hair, and my body on top of hers, skin to skin. We kissed like that for a long time, the unwrapped condom between us like a promise of what would happen next. After a few moments, she shifted her legs so that I sank between them, propping my chest and upper body on the fluffy white pillows behind her head.

"I'm ready," she said.

She didn't have to say it. I knew she was, with every cell in my body. I shut my eyes and concentrated on breathing; I was terrified I would screw up the next few minutes. Inhale. Exhale. Inhale. Exhale. Inhale. Exhale. Inhale…

"Geoff?"

I opened my eyes. My breath came out hard and fast,

and my heart pounded against my ribcage. "What?"

"You look weird. Your face is all red."

"Is it?" I tried to ignore the growing panic in my stomach.

"Are you okay?"

I gulped. "Yeah . . . I am . . . No . . ."

Laine put her hands on my shoulders. "It's okay," she said after a pause. "Are you nervous?"

"No . . ." I started to lie, but I couldn't go through with it. "Yeah, I'm nervous. I am." Her right hand traveled up my shoulder, lightly caressing my skin, and she hooked her fingers around my ear. I held my whole body rigid. "I just . . . I can't."

"Can't what?"

"I can't do this," I said. No one in his or her right mind would turn this girl down, but here I was, doing just that. "I can't."

She pulled back some on the pillows. "You can't?"

I shut my eyes again. "I can't. Not right now. I don't . . . I'm not ready."

Goddamn it. Loser. What a loser. Worse than a loser.

"Just doesn't feel right," I admitted, my lips somewhere in her hair now, my body still above hers, but the magic of this moment broken. I knew I would regret this every day for the rest of my life. It might be my only chance with her, but in the end, it didn't feel right. Not after what had happened between her and Evan; not in a hotel room Evan had paid for in the hope of landing in bed with Laine himself. And not with SNL playing behind us, the blue lights of the TV dancing through the dark room and landing somewhere on the bed. Slowly, my hardness faded away. This moment was over. Way over.

"Do you hate me?" I whispered when she stayed silent.

"No." Her forehead rested against mine. "I could never hate you."

I rolled off of her and propped myself on my elbow. "I wanted to do it. I did. Just didn't feel quite right—"

"It's okay." She yawned and looked at the clock on the bedside table. "12:45 a.m. I'm actually really tired."

I chuckled. "We're supposed to stay up late. Like, all night. It's prom night."

"I know, but I could just fall asleep right now." She yawned again, and curled against me.

"Do you want to get dressed?"

"No." She picked up the remote control and switched off the TV. Darkness flooded the room. "Let's just go to sleep"

SUNDAY, MAY 5

THE TEXT MESSAGE ping on my phone woke me up around seven a.m.

Laine lay sleeping beside me, wrapped in a white sheet, and tucked in the crook of my arm. Twisted pieces of what remained of her up do spread out over the pillow, and she slept with a slight smile of her face. Not wanting to wake her up, it took me five or six minutes to pull my arm out from underneath her body. When I finally did, the arm stung from sleeping in such an awkward position. I disregarded that and fumbled for the phone in my pants pocket. Four text messages from Josh waited for me.

***11:45 PM** Where R U?*
***12:36 AM** Meet us at After Prom. We're already here*
***1:57 AM** Hope U R OK. Getting kinda worried.*
***5:45AM** Holy Shit. Call me.*

Jesus. I must have been in a coma. Well, for at least half of the night, I *had* been pretty distracted. I looked from the phone to Laine, and back again. Whatever Josh wanted, it could wait. This was more important. She was more important. I had fucking slept next to Laine Phillips, and she didn't laugh in my face. She lay in my arms all night. Naked. Vulnerable. In this hotel room. Even after we didn't have sex, she still didn't leave me.

This had been the best night of my life. Thank God I went to prom. Thank fucking God.

Staring at her, I knew I wanted a keepsake—some way to remember that moment. Something to prove to myself that it happened on the days when I didn't believe it. When the phone buzzed in my hand from another text message, it didn't annoy me that time. It gave me the fucking answer to my problems.

I eased back in bed with her, and unlocked the camera on the phone. When the screen came up, I switched it to "selfie" mode, and aligned it as well as I could. She lay next to me in a dead sleep, her arm covering her naked breasts. I snuggled closer to her and snapped the photo. Then I threw the phone back on my pile of clothes and gently put my hands on her stomach. She stirred, nestling her body into me. God, this could have been a scene from an awesome movie, but it wasn't.

This was my fucking life. Awesome.

"Mmmmhhhhph," she said as she opened her eyes.

"Hey, you." She yawned.

"Hey, Laine."

Her neck cracked as she stretched it. "So. What . . . what time is it?"

"It's early. Seven."

She yawned again, and then her eyes widened. "Oh God, seven?"

"Yeah. Seven."

"Shit. Really?"

"Yep."

She sat up, and the bed sheet fell away from her body. My eyes immediately fell on her breasts. God, they were prefect. And I had felt them. Whenever I wanted. All night.

Maybe she'd let me touch them again.

"I'm late," she said. She sounded frantic, and it jarred me out of my daydream. "Oh, God. Curfew." She got out of bed and started looking for her clothes.

"What curfew?" I'd never had one. Mom and David knew I wouldn't do anything reckless, and I never had. Well, not before prom night.

"My parents said to be home at six," she said as she pulled on her underwear. "They said six a.m. on the dot. They didn't know Evan and I were coming here, and I was supposed to just stay half the night so they wouldn't find out."

I got out of bed, and followed her lead. My pants, boxer shorts, and shirt lay in a wilted heap on the floor. They didn't look nearly as James Bond like in the harsh light of morning. Instead, they just looked cheap. Wrinkled. And cliché.

I blew out a long breath and started putting on the

clothes. I also slipped the unwrapped condom back in my pants pocket.

"Are they really strict?"

"Kind of. I should have—I should have called, and told them I was spending the night at Jillian's house." She zipped up her dress, and the action might as well have been a slap across my face. This wasn't midnight with a clock, pumpkin and glass slipper, but it was what seven a.m. looked like on the morning after the best night of my life. Fantasy over. No more dreaming. No more soft, serene sleep next to the pristine princess of my high school.

"God, they're going to kill me." She walked over to the nightstand and fumbled around for the bobby pins and crystal clips that made up part of her hairdo.

"Why don't you just call them now?" I buttoned the last button on my shirt and grabbed my phone, making sure to lock it so she wouldn't see the photo I took of her.

"No, they won't . . . they won't believe me. Not an hour after curfew."

"Okay," I said. "I'll take you home right now."

"Yeah," she said. "That's the best thing."

Questions flooded my mind. Did she think this had all been a mistake? Was last night awful? Did she hate me for backing out on her? Did I look disgusting naked? Had I imagined all of this?

When I reached the hotel room door, she pulled me out of my thoughts with a quick kiss. "Last night was nice, Geoff."

"Nice?"

"More than nice." She opened the door of the room and the vast hallway greeted us. "But now we have to go."

We didn't pay the balance on the room. We didn't even stop by guest services to check out. Whatever. Evan, or his brother, or whoever's name had secured the reservation could pay the balance later.

Laine and I rushed outside to the valet stand, and left as fast as we could. Cincinnati was waking up all around us, and the bright sunlight bothered me. Why couldn't last night have just lasted forever? Why? Why did things have to be like this?

Once again, I drove the BMW as fast as I could manage, but this time for a different reason. We zipped through downtown and across the Big Mac Bridge in less than five minutes. The car didn't hit any red lights this time. Kinda what I expected. We pulled up to her house a mere five minutes after that.

"Do you want me to say anything to your parents?" I asked as I put the car in park by the curb. She hadn't spoken to me the entire drive home. "I could tell them some kind of story, say something . . . er . . . maybe you came over to my house because of Evan . . ."

"No. It won't do any good. They won't believe you. It's my fault for not telling them anything."

"It's not your fault."

She gave me a rueful look. "You know what?"

"What?"

"I left my crown on the table at The Syndicate." She closed her eyes, as if the realization annoyed and disappointed her. "Some Prom Queen."

"I'm sure someone picked it up. Someone will get it

to you." Even as I said it, I felt bad. Of course she'd want that crown. I would have wanted it. What a fail. I should have remembered something like that. Crowns mattered to girls, especially when they won them.

Her eyes drifted open, and when they did, I wasn't sure what I saw. "It's probably in the trash somewhere."

"It's not your fault that you missed your curfew." I just wanted to say anything to make her feel better. God, this morning had turned awkward, and I couldn't figure out how to change that.

"It is my fault, Geoff." She hooked her fingers around the door handle, and when she looked back at me, her eyes had turned cold. "Listen, I had a good time with you last night."

"I did, too." If only I could find the words to really express how I felt at that second, but they didn't exist in the English language.

"A really good time. You're a nice guy."

"It's the blond, bushy eyebrows. That's what did it. They drew you in."

Maybe I should have said more right then. I could have. I had more than a good time. I had a great time, and that night in the hotel was something perfect. Something I might never experience again, no matter how much I wished I could.

She glanced down at her dress, and I had the sudden urge to reach out and grab her for one last kiss. I wanted to do something to tell her how much I thought I loved her, but at that moment, I was too afraid to say anything. Like an idiot. A better man wouldn't have made a dumb mistake like that.

"See you later," she said, as she opened the car door.

She got out, slammed the door behind her, and walked up the brick path to her house. I waited for her to look back at me.

She didn't.

Chapter thirteen

I SAT IN the BMW for a long time after I'd parked the car in the garage. I didn't get out. Didn't move much. Didn't do anything.

On the way home, I turned on my Radiohead playlist and blasted the *OK Computer* album as I drove the car through Robert Hill's central business district, past the Starbucks and by the school. Heritage High School still had the remains of After Prom decorations out on the front lawn, but just like me, they resembled a wilted mess of hope and anticipation. Balloons touched the ground, losing air. Broken streamers littered the front walk. Even the sign saying "Prom to the Stars" had a few missing lights.

Morning-afters didn't look good on anything, or anyone.

"Karma Police" played six times while I sat in the garage before I decided to get out of the car. By then, it was just after eight a.m.

"You might as well go inside, since the fantasy's over," I muttered to myself, as I flipped off the engine. "Can't sit out here all day."

As I got out, I noticed something on the passenger seat. A small bobby pin with a crystal on the end lay tucked between the grooves of leather. No doubt it came from Laine's immaculate prom hairstyle. I picked it up, and put it in my pocket. At least I had some kind of keepsake from the night.

Mom, David, Blake and Bruce had all gathered in the kitchen. When I walked in, Mom stood near the sink, holding a half-washed plate in her hand. Blake, Bruce and David all sat at the bar that jutted out from the kitchen island, with untouched breakfast in front of them. They all stared at the TV, and I noticed they had turned it to the morning news show on FOX.

Odd. They almost never watched the news.

"Hey guys," I said.

"Oh Geoff, oh my God!" Mom looked over at me, jumped, and dropped her plate on the floor behind the cooking island. It crashed against the slate tile and shattered.

David stood up. "You okay, hon?"

"Damn. This is my favorite china," Mom said, now on the floor. "We've been trying to call you, Geoff."

"You have?" I looked down at my phone. Yep, the missed calls were there, right along with the text messages from Josh. I'd been so distracted that I hadn't noticed them. I stepped forward. "Let me help you."

"Watch out Geoff, there's sharp pieces of glass here." Mom looked up at me, and that's when I noticed she'd been crying. Puffy eyes, a red rose, and splotchy forehead gave her away. In fact, I wondered if she might resume crying at any second.

"Mom. What's going on?" I sat back on my heels.

"Oh Geoff, it's just so terrible. I just . . . this is so awful . . . I just can't believe it."

"Believe what?"

"It's all over the news. They've been doing reports all morning, live reports. What's that reporter's name, over at WCPO? Shannon? Or is it Alison?"

"It's the one whose dad was that Bengals Pro Bowler, I think, hon," David said.

"Mom. What are you talking about? Live reports on what?" I glanced at David. "Alison's on the NBC station. And you guys are watching the FOX station. Just so you know."

"It doesn't matter. We've been switching back and forth all morning." Mom shook her head, still obviously upset. "They've all been reporting on it."

"Reporting on what?" I willed her to form a sentence that made sense.

She gulped. "Evan Carpenter. He was in a car wreck last night."

"What?"

"A huge car wreck."

Maybe I didn't hear her correctly. "Car wreck? What?"

"Yes." She paused, and bit her lip. "A drunk-driving accident. It was two cars over on 471. He hit another car, and flipped three times." She swallowed back some of her emotion. "They said he was driving eighty-five miles an hour when he hit the other car. Honey, Evan died. And so did the driver of the other car. He was in his fifties."

"What? Oh my God. Are you serious?"

"Yes." She gulped. "They said he was dead on arrival at the hospital. They didn't even make it to St. Elizabeth around the corner."

"Jesus Christ." My mouth went dry. "He's dead? I can't believe this. There must be a mistake."

"I know, honey. It's so awful."

I leaned up against the stove, and my head started to spin. Above me, the TV hummed as the newscast resumed, but I didn't hear any of the words. All I could think about was Laine. She could have been in that car with Evan. She could have died, too, but she didn't. She didn't die, because she was with me. *Me.* She was with me. And we'd just spent the night almost having sex in a hotel room paid for by Evan. A guy who had just died.

"Oh, honey, I know this is horrible news." My mother said this, but her voice sounded hollow, like she was talking to me through a tin can. A large tear rolled down her face. "So sad. This is just what After Prom was supposed to prevent."

"I had no idea."

"I was so worried about you when you didn't come home last night." Mom reached out, and put her manicured hand on my knee. "I'm so glad you're home now."

"I was out with some friends."

"I guessed that. I hope you had fun."

"Evan had such a bright future," David added. He sounded far away, too. "One of the most sought after recruits for Ohio State next year. Full scholarship. Maybe even the NFL."

"Wow," I managed after a moment. "Terrible news."

"He was my best friend," Blake said.

"Mine too," added Bruce.

I glared at them from my place on the floor. What twits. They mostly hung around Evan during football season, and sometimes they went to the same parties. That was it. I couldn't remember a time when they'd had him over to the house, or went over to his. That friendship was thin at best. But it was just like them to co-opt a tragedy and place themselves at the center.

"I'm gonna go upstairs. Do some thinking." I pushed the small pile of china shards I had gathered over to Mom. "I hope that's okay."

"Oh honey, that's just fine."

"Do you want me to help you clean up the rest of this?"

She shook her head. "I've got it. And there are some muffins on the island. Make sure you grab one before you go up to your room. Apple cinnamon."

"I'm really sorry to hear all this." I said it not because it was how I felt. I said it because it was the only appropriate thing to really say.

With my hands tucked behind my head, I lay on the bed and started up at the wooden beams of the ceiling. For once, I liked the quietness of my room, and the break it gave me from the rest of the house. At least here I didn't have to pretend like I cared for some asshole on the football team who got drunk, slapped the girl I loved, and then died in a car accident he'd caused. An asshole like that didn't deserve my sympathy.

Maybe that was heartless. Maybe it was mean. And maybe it was the wrong way to feel, but, as I lay there, I knew with certainty it was the way I felt. Part of me wished I could remind everyone how awful Evan had acted toward Laine before he died. Too bad people considered it rude to talk badly about dead people. Sometimes society really sucked.

This was one of those moments.

I lay there on the bed for a pretty long time, and I didn't sleep. Instead, my thoughts wandered back to the night before; Laine had looked so beautiful, and she'd felt even better when I held her. I was sure no one would ever feel the way she did, and that anyone I might have from here on out wouldn't compare. It had to be that way, right? Wasn't this what love was?

My phone buzzed in my pocket about a half hour after I lay down. When I pulled it out and looked at it, I had another text message from Josh.

9:05AM Dude, are you home yet?
Me: *Yep.*
Josh: *Why didn't u call?*
Me: *Busy*
Josh: *Can u believe that about Evan?*
Me: *Nope*
Josh: *Did u leave Prom w/Laine?*
Me: *. . .*
Josh: *Holy shit. Holy fucking shit.*
Me: *Not that big a deal.*
Josh: *WTF*

I threw the phone down once more, because Josh didn't need to know all about what had happened the night before. No way. Laine and I had our perfect night. Just the two of us. No one else needed to know details, not even my best friend.

Right?

I got up off the bed and wandered over to my desk in the far corner of the room. I decided to wake up the computer and check Facebook. Always a good plan.

I figured I'd see all kinds of posts about Evan, and it turned out I couldn't have been more right. Facebook announced in my news feed right way that fifteen people had shared the article from the *Cincinnati Enquirer* announcing Evan's tragic death. "Prom King Dies in Tragic Accident," the headline screamed, and it already had about seventy comments on the article. Some people had vague Facebook posts up, talking about "living for every day" and "making every moment count." Others claimed Evan as their best friend or a person they looked up to in life; I read it all with distaste. No matter what people said, I knew the truth about Evan. I saw who he really was at Prom—a coward, an asshole, and a bad person. It didn't mean I wished him dead, but it did mean I didn't have to mourn his death.

I checked Laine's Facebook page last.

"I can't believe this, my heart has broken," it said. Forty-five people had commented on her status, most of them juniors and seniors from school. Over and over again, they told her how sorry they were that she'd lost the love of her life. And that was all. She didn't reply to any of the comments, and after staring at them for about fifteen minutes, I couldn't resist sending her a message myself.

Of course, I did it by direct message.

"Are you okay?" I wrote. "Just call me if you want to talk. I'm thinking about you." Then I sat back and waited for her to reply.

She never did.

MONDAY, MAY 6TH

EVAN'S DEATH STRANGLED the Heritage High School hallways. It sat in every classroom like an unwanted visitor, and wrapped through the hallways like an odor no bleach could destroy. Teachers said grief counselors would come to school all week, then passed out black ribbons to Heritage's six hundred students. We all pinned them to our chests, right above our hearts, and we wore them every day. All four Cincinnati TV stations did live shots for their morning shows and noon newscasts in front of the school, and reporters interviewed a couple of students as they walked from the school parking lots to first period. For the first time in my four years there, Heritage High administrators closed the school doors during lunch, and no one ate off campus.

As soon as I arrived at school the Monday after prom, I searched for Laine. She was all I thought about, all I wanted, all I needed. I could make it through the nightmare of people grieving if I had her to do it with me.

I saw her in the hallway between second and third period. A couple of friends surrounded her and her locker, all with sympathetic looks. They had on black dresses, dark heels and somber expressions, as if they had coordinated their outfits. Laine didn't smile or laugh, either, and her slumped shoulders made me wonder if she had slept at all since that morning at the Cincinnatian Hotel.

I didn't see her at lunch, or in the hallway afterward,

like I always did. In fact, I didn't see her again until AP English. When I walked into class she already sat at her seat with her textbook open, as if she was reading it, and something about the way she sat made me hesitate to talk to her. She didn't look up from the pages at all as everyone else filed into the room, with their usual conversations about homework assignments and the food at lunch. I stood by the door, sized Laine up, and then took my seat in the second row.

"Good afternoon," Mr. Langston said after the bell rang. Just like the students, he wore a black ribbon on his chest, although his was askew and already frayed against a mustard yellow button-down shirt that magnified a ketchup stain on his stomach.

"I have a few announcements to make here, before we get started." He cleared his throat, and picked up a piece of loose-leaf paper from the lectern. "We just got an email that funeral arrangements for Evan Carpenter will be on Wednesday afternoon, at one p.m. at the First Episcopalian Church here in Robert Hill. Visitation is Tuesday from four to eight p.m. at Truitt Funeral Home. Any students wishing to attend the funeral will need to bring a written excuse from their parents." He cleared his throat again. "Now. Does anyone have any questions, or comments?"

"Did they say anything more about the police investigation?" someone asked from the back of the room.

"No." Mr. Langston gripped the sides of the lectern, and his bony knuckles popped out from his chalky white skin.

"Just can't believe he died," I heard someone say across the room.

"Look, I never had the pleasure of teaching Mr. Carpenter, but I know a lot of you were friends of his, or looked up to him. He certainly appeared to have a bright future playing football for the Buckeyes." He paused, and then dramatically shook his head. "It's a shame that will never happen for him. A big shame. And on that note, I need to remind you that the AP test is Friday. Five days. I know for many of you this will be long week, so I suggest you use the rest of this hour to study for the test."

I stifled my groan, as the rest of my classmates opened up their study guides. Mr. Langston's right about this; we were all about to have a long-ass week. I had the AP Calculus test on Wednesday morning, the AP English Language test on Friday morning, AP Biology the following Monday, AP German on the fifteenth, and I would follow that up with European History on the same afternoon.

I needed to get to work, but before I did, I glanced over at Laine. She still didn't look up from her notebook, but I saw her wipe away a few tears.

Chapter fourteen

WEDNESDAY, MAY 8TH

"DAVID," MOM CALLED from just inside the garage. "Are you and the boys ready?"

"We're coming," he yelled from somewhere upstairs.

She clicked the key fob on her Mercedes SUV and turned her sad, sympathetic eyes to me. "So. Are you ready to do this, honey?"

"Yeah, Mom, I am." I leaned up against the garage wall, and put my foot at a ninety-degree angle against it. With my hands tucked into my gray pants, I studied her. She had the strangest expression, as if someone she'd loved and cared for had died, not someone she knew from Friday Night Football, the local news, and gossip shared around the dinner table.

"How long do you and the boys want to stay at the visitation, Geoff?"

I shrugged my answer because in truth, I didn't want to go at all. I didn't want to pay my respects, or honor a person I knew to be a fraud, and an asshole. Evan Carpenter had never been nice to me, not even in kindergarten, and on top of that he'd been even worse to Laine. He didn't deserve anything, but at that moment I was stuck. The whole senior class and most of the rest of the school planned to attend the services. Much of the larger community would be at Truitt Funeral Home that night, too, and David liked to keep up the pretense of prominence.

We had to go, no matter how much it pained me.

"Well, I guess while we wait for them, and um . . . we'll just get in the car," Mom said, motioning for me to follow her.

Once the engine started and she turned her attention to the radio, I decided I might as well admit my misgivings. "Do you really want to go to this?" I asked her.

"Of course I want to go." She looked at me through the rear view mirror. A frown split her smooth forehead into equal parts. "Why do you ask?"

"Evan wasn't all that great of a person, Mom."

"He wasn't?" She didn't look up from the console, but her hand stopped punching buttons.

"No. He wasn't." I paused. "Listen, can I tell you something?"

"Sure you can, honey."

"Evan was a horrible person. Mean. A jerk." I gulped. "He also got so drunk at prom that night that he slapped Laine Phillips, right after she and he became Prom Queen and King."

Her head snapped as she looked over at me, her attention no longer on whatever bothered her on the console. "Slapped her?"

"Yep."

"Are you—are you sure—"

"I'm not lying." I interjected, my annoyance growing.

"In front of everyone?"

"Not in front of everyone, Mom." I leaned my head back against the leather headrest as the memories of that night pushed against my head. "Just me. Well, I think I was the only one who actually saw it. You know, they were off in a corner having an argument, and she was angry—"

"Wait. Laine Phillips." Mom twisted her lips to one side of her face, deep in thought. "Tell me which one that is, again? Is she that cute girl?"

"She's the one that's a model." I closed my eyes, still leaning against the seat. The back of my head began throbbing, and the dull ache snaked down my neck. "Blonde. Tall. Skinny. Really smart." I stopped there, knowing better than to list all of Laine's better qualities, because Mom didn't know anything about my infatuation with her.

"Oh, yes." Mom sighed. "I remember her now. She went to one of the Catholic schools—St. Margaret's."

"Until seventh grade." I turned my head to her, and opened one eye. "Do you have any Tylenol? My head is killing me."

She opened up the console between the seats, and handed me the small bottle she kept in the car. "So he hit her?"

"Yep." I swallowed a couple of the pills. The way this conversation was going, I would need the whole bottle.

She shook her head. "Maybe it was a misunderstanding."

"No way," I said, the headache spreading through the

back of my head. "There was no mistaking it. He meant to hit her."

"So sad." She clicked her tongue. "We have to go to the funeral honey. He's dead." Then she checked her watch. "Do you think they'll come down soon?"

"Why don't you honk the horn?" I said, after I popped two more pills in my mouth. "Listen. It's more than that with Laine. She's not just a kid in my class. We've been—we're—I don't know?"

"What do you mean?"

"We've been sort of dating on and off, I guess." I left the part out about how I almost lost my virginity just days ago to Laine. Mom didn't need to know that. Ever. "In between her dating Evan on and off."

"Did she go to prom with Evan?"

"Yeah," I said bitterly. "She did. And now I just don't know what to do, like if I should try to talk to her about what happened, and then there is the whole slapping—"

Mom's eyes moved from mine to the garage door by the kitchen. I followed her in time to see David, Blake and Bruce walk through the opening door. "Let's talk about this later, honey. After the visitation."

David had to park the SUV in the First Presbyterian Church parking lot, three blocks from Truitt Funeral Home's brick mansion. Everyone in Robert Hill, it seemed, had turned out for the visitation.

Black bunting rimmed the mansion's wide pillars. A long black limo and a black Hearse waited outside the front doors, and visitors who came to pay their respects wound their way down the circular driveway to the sidewalk. Everyone wore black, and many people concealed their faces behind large black sunglasses. We might as well have been at the funeral for a Hollywood celebrity.

The five of us didn't speak to each other as we waited in line. David nodded at people as they walked by, and my mom occasionally gave people a sad smile, but for the most part we stayed silent.

To pass the time, I counted the people in line around us, and got to five hundred by the time we walked to the front door to sign the condolence book. It gave me a nice distraction from beating myself up over the fact that I hadn't felt sad about Evan's death for even a minute.

"There are a lot of people here," I muttered to my mom after I signed my name. "A lot."

"Did you expect anything less, Geoff?" She gave me one of those sideways looks that meant she wanted me to shut up, as she took my hand and led me into the main viewing room.

Low lights and large stands of flowers in the Heritage High School colors of red, maroon, and yellow fanned out from Evan's open casket coffin, which lay at the end of a long row. His family sat in a group of chairs off to the side of the casket. I sucked in my breath when I saw Laine sitting among them, and then I cursed myself because my dick got hard.

What kind of an asshole got hard at a funeral?

I stepped out of line for a moment, shoved my hands in my pants pockets, and forced myself to think about frogs. Frogs weren't sexy; Frogs didn't want to have sex with me, and I didn't want to have sex with frogs. Frogs had beady eyes, and slimy backs. They didn't wear sexy black peplum dresses with black netting across the chest and shoulders to funerals. They didn't smell like bubblegum mixed with flowers and salt. And they didn't toss me sad smiles, have long blonde hair or wear red lipstick.

As we neared the casket, a woman passed out tissues. I handed mine to Mom because she started crying right when we walked in the front door of the funeral home. She was sentimental like that.

"I hate these things," Mom said, under her breath. "Reminds me of your dad."

"Yeah, I know what you mean." Of course, Dad's visitation and funeral didn't have a fifth of the number of people this one did. He'd been such a quiet person, with few friends, but a good reputation. He said he'd liked it better that way, and that being a good person with a giving heart while on earth went further than being a famous one.

"We should say something to his parents," Mom whispered to me, as Blake and Bruce walked with David up to the front of the room. They stood in a row in front of the while casket, and for a moment they reminded me of three male Russian nesting dolls. I had to stop myself from laughing out loud, because it was not a good look for them.

"Okay," I said, because once again it was the proper thing to do. I stepped forward to view Evan's body with Mom. He lay on a while pillow, and had his eyes closed. He wore a blue suit, and someone had nestled his Heritage and Ohio State football jerseys next to his shoulder. He didn't look like he had been in an accident at all.

After a few seconds, Mom pulled me over to the family. Evan's mother, a stocky woman with a severe blonde bob, stood up from her chair. "Thank you for coming," she said, in a voice tortured by years of cigarette smoking. She held onto the back of the metal chair in front of her with one hand, and shook my mom's with the other.

"Of course," Mom replied, in a warm but still quiet voice. "We really are so sorry for you loss."

That was the kind of thing people said when someone died. I'd heard it hundreds of times after my dad passed away, and the words didn't mean anything to me. I'm sure it didn't mean anything to Evan's mother, either, but she still hugged my mom.

"I hate that this happened," I said, as Mrs. Carpenter turned to embrace me. Over her shoulder, though, I locked eyes with Laine. She gave me another sad smile, and all I felt was confused. She hadn't responded to any of the text messages, Facebook messages, or direct messages on Twitter I had sent her since Sunday. And, I admit, I'd sent more than a few.

I'd sent about twenty-five.

Now, seeing her in the funeral home, things had turned even more awkward. My brain swam in a mix of memories about the night we almost had sex, anger at Evan, confusion about her reaction to his death, sadness over the whole thing, and the desire to stand up in front of everyone and tell them the only girl I cared about was Laine Phillips. She didn't belong in the middle of all this, playing grieving girlfriend to a guy who'd disrespected and mistreated her. She belonged with someone like me; someone who would never hurt her like that.

Laine stood up after Mrs. Carpenter had released me, and hugged my mother. Their embrace lasted longer than it should have, and Laine hung onto my mother like a life raft. "Thank you for coming," she said in a muffled voice against Mom's shoulder.

When she turned to me, Laine had a blank look on her face, just like she used to before this all happened. Anyone at this visitation who looked over and saw us would have thought we didn't know each other. The blank expression and dullness behind her eyes wore on me, until I couldn't stand it any longer. Who cared where we were?

Time, once again, to man up.

"I'm worried about you," I said to her in a low voice. I grabbed her arm and gently pulled her closer to me so that only she could hear my next few words. "Really worried."

She glanced at the rest of the receiving line. "Not . . . not here, Geoff. I can't . . . I'm just . . ."

"I know you loved Evan." My hand tightened on her arm, but I held my voice steady. "But I have to talk to you. You can't ignore me anymore."

"I know." She bit her lip. "Tomorrow. Come over tomorrow." She sounded nervous and unsteady, and my heart quickened in my chest. At least, in the middle of all this confusion, I'd get to see her again.

"What time?"

"After seven," she whispered. "That should work. After seven."

"Perfect," I replied.

I didn't say any more, because she'd already turned away from me to greet another mourner at the visitation. She had a role to play, and we both knew it. I walked a few steps away and then turned to watch her. She played the grieving girlfriend so well.

THURSDAY, MAY 9TH

I PARKED THE car and tentatively walked up to the red front door at Laine's house. What if she'd changed her mind? I shut my eyes as I rapped on the door, and prayed she hadn't. I had to talk to her, and I needed to do it that night. It was the only way I could hope to understand her.

The hall light came on, and the front door flew open about fifteen seconds after my last rap. Laine stood behind the door, bathed in the soft glow of a lamp on the hallway table. Her hair hung loose around her shoulders, and the light played up its natural wave. She had on a pair of tan yoga pants and a blue V-neck Xavier University shirt. She made this outfit as sexy as lingerie. All the blood rushed from my face.

"Hey," I said, uncertain. "I hope I didn't disturb you." I felt stupid as I glanced down at my jeans and polo shirt. Why the hell had I dressed as if this was some kind of date? Clearly it wasn't. This was just like me—over thinking everything. I really needed to get a hold of myself. Again. For the ten thousandth time in three months.

"No, it's fine," she replied. She motioned for me to come in, and the closed the door behind me. "I was just studying. I thought maybe you weren't going to come."

Of course I was going to show up. This was Laine Phillips. After all this time, didn't she realize who she was? Had she forgotten prom? Didn't she see what she did to me? Didn't she know what she did to everyone else in school?

"You missed school today," I whispered, trying to control myself, keep myself from coming across creepy.

"I did." She shrugged. "Just couldn't deal with it today, and with the funeral . . . I was studying in the kitchen, just to take my mind off of stuff. So maybe we can study there?"

"Study?"

She smiled. "Yeah. Studying. For the AP English test. That we have tomorrow?"

"Oh, right. That old thing." I'd studied for about five hours for that test, well under my usual. Even that afternoon as I skimmed the study guide while in my room, the words all mushed together like a stew of letters. I couldn't concentrate on any of that. Not with all that had happened recently.

"I guess I should study for that." I hesitated. "But of course, I didn't bring my books or my iPad."

"I guess you're lucky that I have to take the test tomorrow, too." She turned and sauntered down the hall, clearly expecting me to join her. I let my eyes fall on her butt for a couple of seconds before I did. She had one of those great ones, round and perky. The tan yoga pants hugged it in a certain way, and I wondered if we'd get much studying done at all.

Not that I showed up hoping to study.

"Do you want something to drink?" she asked once we reached the small kitchen. She opened up the refrigerator door, and pulled out a Diet Coke. I took a seat at one of the barstools tucked underneath the granite countertop that jutted out like an "L" from the sink. A couple of open books and Laine's iPad littered the top.

"Sure, I'll take one, too. Looks like you've been really working hard here."

"Whatever, it's all running together at this point."

"Yeah, for me, too. I guess I just thought maybe it'd be tough for you to study, because of Evan."

"Right. Evan. God, it's like he's everywhere," she said, as she poured the drinks into two glasses. "I'm glad you came over, because now we have a chance to talk."

"Yeah," I said, thinking of prom night. "We do need to talk."

She sat down on the other bar stool, and handed me a glass. "So," she said after a moment, "prom night was . . . something."

I gulped down half of my drink, but even as I did, my mouth ran dry from anticipation. "Okay. What do you mean?"

"Nothing bad. Just that I didn't want it to end."

"Well, neither did I."

"But it's bad that I feel that way, Geoff." Her left hand swiped at a single tear that fell down her cheek. "We were having so much fun that night, and, while we were, Evan was lying on the side of the highway in a car crash."

"He died instantly. They said so on the news."

"It's just so—so wrong of us." She looked away, and her eyes fell on something in the kitchen. I didn't try to figure out what. "My parents weren't mad when I came home, in case you wondered about that. They were more upset than anything else. Of course, they knew all about Evan's accident."

"I'm not sorry about prom, Laine. I would do it again the same way. Even if I knew what happened next. I mean, what happened next with Evan."

"Geoff, I've been so confused . . ."

"Confused?"

"I wanted Evan to figure himself out, and get better.

Stop being so angry all the time. I didn't want him to die. And now it doesn't feel right that I like you so much."

I narrowed my eyes at her. "Let me ask you something. Why did you sit down next to me in the library that day?"

She smiled. "Back in January?"

"That's the one."

Laine cocked her head, like she was thinking of it. While she did, I held my breath, and it occurred to me just how much I really wanted to know the answer to this question. Why hadn't I asked her before? Why did it take something so drastic for me to really talk to her?

"Because you looked safe."

"I looked safe?" I choked the words out. "Me?"

"Evan exploded in the breezeway at school. I was late meeting him, and he yelled at me then told me to fuck off. I was supposed to give him a ride home, but he got one from Monica. That was the second time he'd yelled at me like that." She broke off, and put her head in her hand. Her fingers covered her face and muffled her next words. "The first time he yelled at me that way, it ended with Evan punching my arm instead of my bedroom wall."

"Holy shit, Laine."

She didn't look up from her hand. "I walked by the library, and when I looked through the glass doors, I saw you. And you looked so nice. So different than Evan."

I snorted, and she pulled her head from her hand. "Come on. Really? I'm nobody."

"You're somebody, Geoff. Everyone is somebody."

My thoughts raced through every second of that afternoon in the library. "But you didn't seem like you'd just been yelled at."

"What can I say?" She gave me a sad smile. "I'm good at hiding things. Faking it. That's my specialty."

"Well, yeah, but it's really sad you went through all this," I said, still in disbelief about what she'd said. Out of instinct, I reached out and placed my hand on her shoulder. "And no one ever came running to me—"

Her rosebud lips twisted. "First time for everything." She inhaled a huge breath. "You're the one person at Heritage High who sees me for who I am. You're the one person who lets me be myself. You never ask me to be someone I'm not. And you're funny."

I sat back, stunned. If I'd known that was all it took, I'd have asked her out years ago, instead of waiting for life to throw us together during the final few hours of high school. Jesus Christ. Was that the secret to this whole thing? Was that the secret to her?

"You don't care about image," she continued. "Well, at least, not when it comes to me. And when I'm with you, I'm relaxed."

"I'm relaxed when I'm with you, too." It might have been an overstatement on my part, but it sounded good in my head. It sounded like something someone would say in a movie, which was kinda of the way life made me feel at that moment.

She looked down at the tile floor. "When I got home and my parents said Evan died, I didn't know what to do. Part of me still had feelings for him . . . and I felt horrible about it because I had just almost had sex with you, so I just decided I wouldn't do anything. I know he wasn't a good person in the end, but he's dead. And that makes it all feel different." She sighed, then got up and walked over to the fridge. She opened it and then fiddled around inside, like whatever it offered her would be the key to everything in life.

I got up and followed her after a couple of seconds. "Look, Laine, let me tell you something. I'm not really good at this stuff."

She turned around, an unopened Diet Coke in her hand. "I'm not really great at this either. Evan's the only I've even been with."

"Maybe it's time to be with someone else."

"Who? You?" She bit back a smile.

"Yeah. Me." I swallowed. "You should be with me, Laine. I won't treat you the way he did. Ever." I reached out and put my hand on the door, closing the door and boxing her against it at the same time. "You're really gorgeous."

She rolled her eyes. "Some people have said that."

"Well, even if you don't believe them, you are."

"So what are you saying?"

"Why don't you give us a chance? You might like it."

She stood so close to me now, and that familiarity of her washed over me as the whole world fell away from us. Nothing else counted, nothing else existed beyond the two of us. Her eyes seduced me, her mouth invited me in, and her steady breath promised me that if I made the leap, I'd find more inside her than I ever wanted.

Before I knew it, my mouth found hers for a hard, fervent kiss. This kiss was about more than just sex. This kiss was a promise. It was a statement from me to her, and from her to me. We didn't have just one late night hookup after a bad night at prom. We had much more than that.

"Let's go outside," she said in a breathy voice, as she broke the connection. "It's a really nice night."

Chapter fifteen

MOMENTS LATER, WE took a seat on the overstuffed wicker couch on the patio. It faced the garden and small pool in the back yard, and a privacy fence surrounded the perimeter. Out here, we were just as alone as if we were inside. Off in the distance, I heard the occasional rumble of a car engine rolling down the street.

"You don't know what it's like," Laine said.

"I don't?"

"No."

She sank back against the pillows as I perched on the edge of the sofa, angled at her. I didn't touch her, even though I was desperate to. *Desperate.* Instead, I held my body rigid, and my elbows rested on my knees. As I stared at her, I tried to process what had happened in the kitchen. I still tasted that sweet bubble gum flavored lip-gloss, and I was dying to taste it again.

What did I have to do to make that happen?

"No one knew that Evan had an anger problem," she said. "I never told anyone. And I think I was the only one who saw it—until prom night." She turned her head, and focused on something out in the yard. "So stupid."

"How many times did he hit you?" I swapped the word "fucker" for "he" right before I spoke.

"Come on, Geoff—"

"No, Laine. How many times?"

She laughed once without humor. "Other times? What do you mean?"

"You know what I mean. That time at prom wasn't the first time. Even I could tell that."

She shut her eyes as if that would make whatever she had to say next easier. "One other time."

"One other time?" I narrowed my eyes at her as I thought about our conversation on the sidewalk outside of The Syndicate on the night of the prom. "One other time?"

She must have heard disbelief in my voice, because when she opened her eyes, she looked away. She picked up a stray leaf from the mess of pillows next to her and crunched it with her fingers. "Okay. Three other times, besides that. But it wasn't like that. Not like it was that night at prom. He was just so drunk, and he went over the top. And now he's dead, and I just feel so—"

"He shouldn't have hit you. Ever."

"He's dead."

"Doesn't mean he was a nice guy. You can still be a bad person after you're dead."

"I know, but you have to understand something, Geoff. Evan was my first love. My first . . . everything. He was a great boyfriend in the beginning, but he changed this year, after he got into Ohio State. Like, he thought he was invincible or something. And then with the divorce . . . he wasn't the same guy at all."

"It's not your fault he died."

"Isn't it?" She sniffled, and her voice broke a little. "I should have stopped him, or told someone. I could have told one of the teachers he'd hit me; that would have stopped him from ever getting in the car. And now everyone thinks that I'm a horrible person because I didn't stop him, and because I wasn't with him when he died."

"No one thinks that," I said. "No one. They don't blame you."

"I hear what people are saying." She sniffled again, and I thought I saw the beginning of tears in her eyes. "They talk. About him. About me. That's all they talk about right now at school."

"I haven't heard anything."

She answered me with another rueful laugh. "You're not listening. That's the problem. Jesus, Geoff . . ."

How could I convince her? She carried this pain around like a backpack weighted with stones.

In the soft light from the porch she reminded me of a glassy, delicate, fragile angel. I wanted to hug her, tell her she didn't have any guilt when it came to Evan's death. I reached out and took her hand, pulled her up off the pillows and closer to me. She didn't fight me, and, before I knew it, I'd wrapped my arm around her waist. My breath came out heavy and hard in my chest. "You aren't the reason he died." I touched my forehead to hers. "He died because of himself. His own stupidity. Not yours."

"God, a car wreck like that—I just can't—" She broke off, and tucked her head against my shoulder.

"He did it to himself. No one made him get in the car drunk, turn it on, and drive. He did that."

"I thought I loved him once, and I'm not kidding about that. I really did." Her words were muffled against my shoulder. "Now I just feel so bad."

"Everyone does."

"I could have stopped him, even after he hit me. I knew he was drunk."

"This isn't your fault, Laine," I whispered, as I gently pulled her head away from my chest so I could see her eyes again. God, she was so damn hot, even when she cried. "But the way he treated you—that wasn't love. I just wish you would see that for what it was."

I couldn't control myself any longer. My lips found hers, and I kissed her. Just once, and just enough to remind myself that the kiss against the fridge hadn't been some kind of crazy dream that would leave me disappointed when I woke up alone in my bed. It might not have been appropriate, but I did it anyway, and when I broke the kiss her expression told me she liked it, too.

"You deserve someone better than that, Laine."

"I used to think I had it all figured out," she mumbled. "But I don't."

"Me neither." I gave her a small smile. "But I think that's okay. We're only eighteen."

"Eighteen. Wow." She chuckled. "Just kids."

"But legally adults. I just don't feel like one."

"I still can't believe I turned eighteen last December."

"Well, then," I said against her mouth. "I turned eighteen in November. I'm older than you, so you have to listen to me."

We kissed again, deeper and slower this time. I tried to savor it, as my lips and tongue explored her mouth. She moaned, and I knew then that she wouldn't fight me. The pace of our kisses quickened, and seconds later I was on top of her, furiously kissing her lips, mouth, jaw, nose, cheek, whatever I could find. I wanted every part of her at all at once, and she seemed the same way, pulling me harder against her hips as she moaned my name. We stretched out on the couch, her legs wrapped around my hips, and the pillows fell away from us as our bodies locked in a hard embrace.

That wasn't the only thing that got hard.

"I want you," she said after she broke away, panting.

"You do?"

"Yep."

"But what about—"

She held up her hand to stop me from talking. "Forget about that. I just want you."

"I want you too," I said against her ear. "I always have."

"Not just like that, Geoff. I want you now."

I held myself above her. "Right here? Now? On the patio?"

"Right here."

I cocked my head, unsure I understood what she meant. "Wait. You mean right now?"

She giggled, and moved her hand down to the hem of her shirt. She moved out from under me, and then pulled off the shirt. All I saw was a red lace bra.

"Yes. On the patio. No one will see us. Mom won't be home for at least an hour."

"Are you sure?"

"Do you still have that condom in your wallet?"

My breath hitched, and my eyes lost focus. The only thing better than having sex with her at a fancy hotel would be having sex with her, right then. Sex right now, on this patio, would mean more. It would mean she didn't regret prom night, that I didn't have some kind of bizarre lottery luck that only struck once. I couldn't believe this. She didn't feel weird about prom night, or, if she did, it didn't bother her enough to push her away from me for good.

"Yeah, I have a condom in my wallet," I finally managed. My nerves got the best of me, and I snickered.

"Good deal, Geoff." She raised an eyebrow at me. "I'm glad you came prepared."

"Well after Prom night . . ." I shrugged. "I figured . . . but then I didn't know . . ."

"Geoff." She interrupted me.

"What?"

"Shut up," she demanded. "Kiss me."

Who was I to turn her down?

FRIDAY, MAY 10TH

WHEN YOU SPEND the night before the AP English Language exam having sex with the hottest girl in school instead of studying, it's impossible to do well on the test. All you do is relive every moment of it in your head. Every kiss. Every time your lips grazed her boobs. The shiver she had when your mouth traveled down her flat stomach. Every time you touched her clit. The warmth you felt when you slid inside her. The way she said your name. How it felt to come inside her. The delicious thrill of the afterglow.

At least, that's what happened to me.

I wrote it into the test. The words for the multiple

choice questions danced on the page, until every one of them looked like questions for a sex test in *Maxim*. The essay portion was even worse. I had to read and then re-read every question in the book, afraid I'd start writing an essay about how awesome Laine looked naked. I'd never been happier to have an eraser on the end of my pencil, and by the end of the test, I wondered if anyone else felt the sexual charge in the room. She sat four rows away from me, and glanced at me every few minutes. Sometimes, she smiled. Being in the same room with her was torture—delicious, sweet torture that left me gripping the desk, and clenching my pencil so tight that I broke two of them during the first hour.

I would be lucky to get a three on this exam. Very lucky. I had to get a three to get three hours of college credit at UVA, and a five to get the chance to have six. Earlier in the year, I'd planned on studying so hard I'd get a five on all the tests. I even told people I'd get those grades, because I suffered from overconfidence. I used to care so much about stuff like that, but it didn't matter that day, because suddenly I had Laine Phillips. School wasn't everything. Not anymore. She was.

And apparently, Laine wanted the rest of Heritage High to know.

"Can I sit with you guys at lunch?" she asked Nathan, Josh and I, as we walked out of the classroom after class. Drained and disillusioned from the test, I didn't hear her at first. In fact, Nathan's mouth dropping open was the only way I knew she'd said something at all. He stopped in the hallway around the corner from Mr. Langston's classroom, and we halted with him.

"You want to sit with us," Nathan replied, making

both a question and statement. "Us."

"Sure." Laine had a crazy smile on her face, and she hooked her arm into mine. Josh snickered as she looked from him to me. "Is that okay?"

"But why?" Nathan still had the quizzical look on his face, but I didn't blame him. He didn't know much about what happened after prom, so Laine's question had to surely come as something of a shock.

"Why not? I mean, Geoff and I are—"

"Um . . . yeah. It's fine." He frowned, shifted his backpack on his shoulders, and looked at me as if I had just won $200 million bucks in the lottery. "Are you sure you want to . . ."

"Nathan. Come on. It's fine. She can sit with us," I said, growing bolder every second Laine's arm stayed linked with mine. "Whatever."

"Is it all right that Allison is going to sit with us, too?" Josh asked. He sounded like a courtier asking permission from the Queen of England, and I had to hold back my laughter.

"Allison. Allison Nichols?" Laine asked. "Sure. She should sit with us. Why not?"

I jerked my head in the direction of the cafeteria, aware that this was going to cause a stir in that jungle. Honestly, I couldn't wait for that. Already, I was getting looks from some of the underclassman who'd noticed that Laine had her arm linked with mine. Evan, be damned. Okay, maybe that wasn't a nice thing to think right at that moment. I just couldn't help myself.

Laine made me forget my manners. Among other things.

"Come on." I clasped my hand in hers. "Let's do it."

The six of us sauntered in the cafeteria about five minutes later. Josh had picked up Allison and her angst at her locker on the way, so the six of us made a spectacle as we walked through the wide double doorway of the lunchroom, and down the steps to the lunch line. Kids stopped what they were doing. They stopped eating. They stopped talking. They just stared at our group, as if we were some kind of social science experiment gone very, very wrong. Silence covered the room for about fifteen seconds, and then all the kids resumed what they were doing at once.

Strange.

"Well," Allison said, as we filed into a single line for the food, "now they know." She nodded at Laine. "Hope you enjoyed that."

"Oh, I did," Laine said, still holding my hand. "I'm sure everyone will have something to say about this."

"Especially because of what happened with Evan." Allison leaned up against the wall, and crossed her arms. "I mean, did you love him, or anything?"

Laine's face fell. "Yeah. I thought I loved him, but I don't. I was . . . well . . . I was wrong."

"Wrong."

"It wasn't love," Laine told Allison. "It was something else, I think."

"I'm sad that he died," Allison said. "But he wasn't a really super nice guy." She shrugged. "He always treated me like trash. I know you're not supposed to say bad things about dead people, but it's true. That's how he was."

I gawked at Allison for a second. It was the first time I'd heard some else verbalize just how I felt about Evan.

"That's okay," Laine said, as she reached for a tray.

"I miss him, of course, but he wasn't very nice to me, either."

"What line are you getting into?" I asked her. "Salad bar or hot bar?"

She didn't even look, just kept her eyes on me. "Hot bar. After that test, I'm hungry for pizza."

SATURDAY, MAY 11TH

BLAKE, BRUCE AND I sat in a semi-circle around the kitchen table. Instead of the usual housework and chores, David had given me the day off to study for the three AP tests I had coming up the following week. The only caveat to the whole thing was that while I studied, David expected me to make sure Blake and Bruce spent their Saturday morning studying, too. While I had major tests that would determine how much time and money UVA would take from me in the next four years, they had finals, too. Both of them needed to do well. Their grades had improved quite a lot because of my tutoring, but their averages still rested on their test scores.

They were not happy about this.

"So what do you want us to do next, Professor?" Bruce asked me, with a voice dripping in sarcasm. He had just made the last flashcard of terms for his government final, and a huge pile of cards with info on Congress, Supreme Court cases, famous presidential decisions, and more, and they all lay in front him.

"Now that you have the cards, you need to study them," I said calmly. I didn't look up from the AP European History study app on my iPad. I knew when he wanted to bait me into a fight, and his voice sounded like he wanted to do just that.

"Study them how?"

I looked up. "Review them, go over the facts, and test yourself."

"Review them, go over the facts, and test yourself." Bruce mimicked me in a baby voice as he shuffled the cards through his hands. Blake didn't say anything, preferring to watch the two of us play out whatever happened next.

"You know, you don't always have to be so rude," I said in a quiet, even voice. As I talked, my phone buzzed in my pocket. Once I pulled it out of my pants, I read a text message from Laine on the front screen.

Laine: *R U studying?*
Me: *Yep*
Laine: *Me too. Bored. Wish I was with you.*
Me: *Soon*

Blake's voice pulled me away from what I wanted to type next. "Who's that, Geoff?"

"No one," I said, tossing the phone down. "And you know what? I'm not the one who's rude. That's you. And you're the one who needs my help."

Bruce laughed, and continued his shuffling. He handled the stack of index cards like a dealer in an underground poker game. "Oh, let me tell you, you piece of shit. I don't need your help."

"Your grades need my help."

Blake giggled, and Bruce shot him a withering glare.

"Shut up."

"Shut up?"

"Yeah, shut up, you pissant." He looked from me to his twin brother, as if he wanted backup from Blake. On cue, Blake nodded vigorously.

"Why all the hate?" I asked Bruce, bringing his focus back to me. "Seems like you've been drinking a lot of haterade lately."

"Nope." Bruce let the gentle rhythm of the cards break up his words. "Wouldn't call it haterade. I just don't like what I see. And Evan was our friend."

I rolled my eyes. "Oh please, don't start with this bullshit. Somebody dies, and everyone starts running around saying they were friends with the person."

"We were friends," Blake replied.

"Right. You guys went to a couple of parties together, and played on the same football team. Real deep friendship."

"You don't know anything about friendship," Bruce said, as he pushed his chair back from the table. The scrape added shrillness to his words. "Since you have none."

"I have plenty."

"Yep, I believe that one."

"Evan was a cool dude," Bruce replied. "You didn't see him the way I did." He gestured to his brother. "The way we did. Such a fun guy on the football team. I looked up to him."

I snorted, and Bruce's jaw hardened.

"Evan was going through a tough time the last couple of months. Lots of stuff with his family. It was hard for him," Bruce muttered. "He tried to hide it, but we knew.

Just wish we could have helped him more."

"You wouldn't understand," Blake said, and his voice broke a little bit. It was the first time I'd heard real pain in his voice in a long time. The first time I saw something beyond the anger and disgust of my stepbrother. To tell the truth, hearing the pain in his voice bothered me.

"I'm sorry," I said.

"Sure you are," Bruce said, and just like that, the animosity had returned.

"Just tell me this, Blake," I said. "Why do you hate me so much?"

"Simple. Because you're perfect. Because our dad loves you more than he loves us. And because you think you're better than us."

"What?" I asked, shocked.

"That's what I think." Blake stood up from his chair, and glanced at his brother. "You coming?"

"Hold on. We haven't finished the tutoring," I protested, suddenly worried I might not get paid by David for that week if the twins bailed on my help.

"Whatever. I'm done." Bruce scooped his books and papers off the table with one swoop of his arm. He gave his brother one more glance. "I'll see you downstairs?"

"Um . . . yeah . . ." Blake struggled to find other words. "Yeah."

With a nod, Bruce turned and stormed out the door. When I glanced back to his brother, Bruce's face was ashen. "What the hell? What did I ever do to you guys? You treat me like I'm the hired help, and I don't fucking deserve this shit."

Blake stood up and nodded. "Maybe not. We have kinda been a little bit hard on you."

"Understatement of the fucking year." I rolled my eyes.

"It's mostly Bruce that hates you, not me"

"Could have fooled me."

"He's very jealous of you, and it's gotten worse in the last couple of months." Blake grabbed his pens and paper. "Just don't cross him again, Mr. Encyclopedia," he said, after a quick reshuffle of his papers.

"I'll remember that." Now it was my turn to stand up from the table. "Whatever. I'm going upstairs. Tutoring's over for the day." I walked away, leaving my phone, schoolbooks, and iPad on the table.

SUNDAY, MAY 12TH

LAINE CAME OVER that afternoon. Her idea, not mine. She said she wanted to study for the other upcoming AP exams, which still loomed over us like large boulders we had to move before graduation. The more I thought about it, the more I realized it sucked that these tests marred our last week of high school. We should have been celebrating, the way half the class already was at school. All they had to get through to make it to graduation were some bullshit finals teachers gave out to prove they taught up to the last day of class.

"Are you home alone?" she asked when I opened the front door. As usual, she had a huge grin on her face, and she wore a black cotton sundress with a halter neck. "I didn't see any other cars in the driveway."

"Yep." I stepped aside to let her in the house. "Mom

and David took Blake and Bruce to the Reds game. Diamond seats."

Earlier in the week, I'd been bummed that they'd bought the twins such expensive tickets to the game as an early graduation gift. Diamond seats cost $250 a piece, and those two idiots didn't deserve an afternoon of endless buffet and seats so close they could spit on the home plate if they wanted. Mom tried to justify it by telling me Blake and Bruce had earned them, because of their improved GPA. Bullshit. It had ticked me off to no end to find out that's what my parents decided to give them. Why didn't they give me something like that for my grades?

But now, I rethought my frustration. An afternoon at Great American Ballpark for them meant an afternoon alone with Laine Phillips for me.

"Diamond seats? Wow." She gave me a quick peck on the lips, as she walked into the foyer.

"Yep." I rocked back and forth on my feet, suddenly nervous again. I closed the front door behind her. "So. Do you still want to study?"

"Sure." She glanced around the wide entryway. "So? Where's your room?"

"Upstairs," I nodded in the direction of the staircase.

For the first time in a long time, the privacy of my room made me thankful. Once we got upstairs, the heavy wooden door shut out the world, as if she and I had some kind of special place all our own. And trust me, when the hottest girl around wanted to spend time with just you, all you wanted was a room like that. Lucky me.

"Your room is huge." She dropped her green messenger bag on the wooden floor and plopped onto the bed, where she bounced, twice. "Really. It's kinda awesome.

Like an apartment."

"Yeah, they leave me alone up here."

Still cautious, I took a seat next to her on the edge of the bed. Did she really want to study? I sure didn't. I wanted to have sex with her again. The word jumbled around in my head, squeezing out other thoughts and making me forget that I had grades to make and tests to study for that afternoon. Maybe I needed to flip on the radio so we had some mood music. Maybe she wanted me to grab her and throw her onto the bed, like something out of a movie. And maybe it was neither. I couldn't figure it out, so I did nothing.

"Honestly, I really used to hate it," I said, looking around at the full-sized bed, the bare desk, the TV on the far side of the room, and the small couch. "I always figured they shut me away up here to get rid of me after Mom married David.

"David hates me. Well, maybe not hate. But he doesn't like me." I shook my head. "Actually I don't know, anymore."

"What do you mean?"

"I thought he hated me for a long time, but my mom told me right before prom that he doesn't. I just—I wish I knew."

She clicked her tongue, as if in thought. "You haven't talked to him?"

"No." I stared at her for a moment, and couldn't think of anything worthwhile to add, so I changed the subject. "You ready for this week?"

"Well, I guess I know the material as well as I ever will. I can't believe this is our last week of high school."

"I know." I gulped, surprised at myself, and the confusion I felt over the upcoming week.

For almost twelve years of school I'd wanted to get away from these people, graduate, and get on with my life. I started talking about UVA back in the sixth grade, telling them I wanted to major in history and be an attorney in Washington DC, like I had some kind of destiny. I sleepwalked my way through school, worshiped Laine from afar, and disregarded everyone else except Nathan, Mark and Josh. Now, in the span of three weeks, everything had changed. Laine and I had had sex. School would end in five days, and I was more conflicted about going to Charlottesville than I ever had been, especially since it meant I had to leave the most amazing girl I had ever met at the end of the summer.

"It's been a weird year," Laine admitted. She shivered, and I reached out my hand to steady her.

"I wouldn't take anything back, Laine." Then I paused. "Except for maybe Evan's death."

She answered me with a sad smile, and a long, deep breath. "Yeah, I know. I wish that had never happened, too." She paused. "But I'm happy we started hanging out, Geoff. Really happy."

"You mean that?"

"Yeah." Now her smile turned genuine. "I really do mean it."

I kissed her right then, because it seemed like the natural thing to do after she'd said something like that. My tongue made its way inside her mouth a half-second later, and we kissed on the bed as I propped all my weight on one arm and ran my other hand along the delicate skin between her jaw, earlobe, and the back of her neck. She moaned once, then twice in between kisses before she fell back on the bed, and I climbed on top of her. Her blonde hair fanned out on the bed and we moved together as she opened herself up to me. We stayed that way for another ten minutes or so in a frenzied make-out, until she broke away and smiled at me with her eyes.

No one in the world had ever looked hotter. No one.

"You're a nice guy, Geoff."

"Maybe." My hand hovered above the ties around her neck as I contemplated undoing them. "Do you want to?"

"Yeah, I do." She swallowed. "Didn't you think we would?"

"Well . . . I mean . . ."

She fidgeted underneath me. "Do you have some?"

My jaw went slack. Of course I didn't. I'd used the only one I had the previous time we had sex. My thoughts raced. I was frantic to come up with a solution. Then I had it. I hopped off the bed. "Give me a second."

I ran down the steps from the second floor as fast as I could, tripped on two, recovered, and then sprinted to the bathroom that David and Mom shared. For once, David's chores had an unexpected bonus. Inside the bathroom, I ripped open the cabinet below the his-and-hers sinks, and fished around the back. Half a second passed before my hands found the box I remembered from the twice-monthly cleaning I gave their bathroom.

Trojan Bare Skin condoms. Sounded legit. Not like I knew any better, though. Shrugging, I grabbed one, threw the box back in the cabinet, and slammed the door shut. As I jogged back up the stairs, I tried to slow my breathing. Laine might be ready to have sex with me, but I still wanted to look suave.

If I could.

"Whoa," I said as I reached the top of the stairs. She lay on the bed, propped up by her elbows, naked. Well, not naked. She still had on a flesh-colored strapless bra and bikini underwear, but both of those left very little covered. Laine should have been on the cover of *Maxim*, but she was in my bed.

"Did you find some?"

"Yeah." I held it up, sandwiched between my index and middle finger. "One."

"Good." When I didn't move from the edge of the steps, she tilted her head. "What are you? . . . Um, don't you want to . . .?"

"Yeah, I do. I just think you look hot," I replied.

She laughed. I loved that laugh. I wanted to hear it forever.

Chapter sixteen

THURSDAY, MAY 16TH

WHEN I DROVE up to school, Laine and her friends already stood in the school parking lot, talking in a semi-circle. They reminded me of a clump of lollipops, with their brightly colored backpacks, meticulous hairstyles, and designer jeans. In the sea of restless students ready for summer break, these girls stood out because they had the kind of self-assured, attention-grabbing aura that repelled and attracted the rest of the student body.

Laine called over to me once she saw me get out of the car, and I couldn't hide my smile as I walked to her. Okay, I may have sauntered, not walked. Do you blame me?

"Hey, Geoff," she said after a quick peck on my lips in front of her friends. "You having a good morning?"

"Yeah." I hooked my arm around her shoulders,

slinging my hand underneath the thick strap of her backpack.

Glancing at her friends was interesting, to say the least. Jillian's confused frown mirrored the expression of disgust on Monica's face.

After a beat, Jillian shrugged. "So. It's like that now? You guys are . . . together. Like . . . together."

"Yep," Laine replied.

"Confirmed. Like for real." She still sounded confused. "That wasn't just a rumor?"

"Nope," Laine said, not dropping the smile from her face. "You guys know Geoff, right?"

"Sure we do." Jillian twisted her mouth, and one of those weird, dramatic expressions crossed her face. "But what about Evan, Laine?"

Laine stepped a little bit closer to me. "What about him?"

"Like, I mean—"

"Evan just died," Monica said, and I recoiled from the anger in her voice. She was a pointy-faced girl who almost never talked to anyone, outside of her clique. "What do you think you are doing?"

"Shut up!" Laine replied. "I'm so sick of this. I'm sorry Evan died, but he wasn't the guy you thought he was. He just wasn't." She pulled even closer to me. "We weren't happy for a long time. He didn't love me."

Monica snorted. "What? And Geoff Miller does? This guy?"

"Why do you care?"

"Evan was your boyfriend for two years, Laine! Doesn't that mean anything to you?"

"Of course it did," Laine replied, not wavering. "But

these last few months, he wasn't the same guy he was when we started dating. He changed after he got into Ohio State."

"You're just saying that because you want it to be okay that you're with Geoff now." Monica said my name the same way some people would say the name "Osama Bin Laden."

"Hey, wait a second," I said, about to jump in and defend myself. "Is that really—"

"Don't be a bitch, Monica." Laine squeezed my hand. "And I'm not just saying that about Geoff. It's true. That's how Evan was."

If someone had wanted to gather up all the anger and suspicion that surrounded the five of us at that moment, they could have bottled and sold it.

"So . . ." I rocked back and forth on my heels, trying to think of something innocuous to say that would break up the building tension. "Everyone ready for graduation?"

Monica rolled her eyes. "I'm sure we're not as ready as you are."

"I guess." I looked down at Laine. "I need to write my speech."

Jillian snickered. "I heard Nichole saying she wrote hers last month."

"I'm sure she did." I nodded in the direction of the front door. "So, do you want to go inside?"

Laine hooked her arm with me and smiled. "Of course."

We should have known something was up when we walked in the front door of Heritage High. I expected the other students to stare and mock us, but this was altogether different. Whole groups of underclassmen fell silent as we walked up the wide staircase in front of the auditorium, and made our way through the hallway full of sophomore lockers. Some students whispered to each other, and after about ten kids did this, Laine tossed me a confused look. I tried to shrug it off, but I caught a few furious, disgusted glares, and heard more than one person call Laine a slut.

Then I saw why.

"Oh shit," I said, as Laine and I rounded a corner near the science wing of classrooms. I dropped her hand and stopped walking. A large white flyer hung on every single locker in the hallway. Someone had printed a large, grainy photo on every single one, a photo I recognized instantly. "Prom Night for The Princess: Sleeping Around While Her Boyfriend Dies" was written in big, bold letters underneath the photo. It might has as well have been the headline on a supermarket tabloid.

"What is this?" Laine yelled. "What the hell is this?" She pushed a freshman out of the way, and ripped the flyer off the nearest locker. There were just a few students there, but the whole hallway fell silent. A couple of other students stepped away from us, giving us space. Every student at Heritage High had seen this photo, or would see it before the bell for first period rang.

"Oh, holy fuck," I said, as shock flooded every blood vessel in my body. "Oh my God."

"You took a picture of me in the hotel on prom night?" Laine looked from me to the flyer, and back again. "Geoff, What is this? If this is some kind of joke—"

"It's not."

"Where did you get this?"

"Get what? The flyer? Laine, it's not—"

"How could you do this?" she shouted, her words directed right at me this time. Her eyes grew wider, almost crazed. She ripped one of the flyers in half, and then another. "Seriously, Geoff, how could you do this to me?"

"I didn't do it. I didn't make that flyer. Why would I do something like that?"

"I'm not fucking talking about the flyer!" She ripped a few more of them off from nearby lockers. "How could you take a picture of me topless like this?" One of the freshmen snickered, and she glared at him. Then she lowered her voice. "How could you?"

"Well, I wasn't—" In the end, I just broke off, and didn't really offer up an explanation. She looked so mad, so furious, I knew there was no way she'd listen to me anyway. I leaned one hand up against the locker and closed my eyes, as a headache started to pound at the base of my neck. "I know who did it."

"Who?"

"Blake and Bruce," I muttered. "Had to be. They're the only ones who could have gotten their hands on my phone, besides my parents." I shook my head as it all became clear. I'd left the phone on the table that day after tutoring. And I hadn't locked it up.

Goddamn it!

"They must have found the photo on the phone."

I was going to kill them. No doubt. It was one thing to just hate me, but to bring Laine into this was totally ridiculous. Unbelievable. Un-fucking-real. This was so the way my life worked, and I hated everything about it. Just when I had a chance to be happy, just when things were going right, those assholes had to go and do this . . .

"What do you mean they found it?" Laine's voice brought me back to the present, and her face grew redder with every question. "What the hell? Why? Why did you take a picture like this? Did you tell them about prom?"

"I didn't tell them! They found the picture and decided they knew what happened."

"Why would you have done something like this and then not deleted the photo?"

"I don't know. I just wanted—I didn't think—it was just supposed to be a picture for me. Just me."

"I trusted you." Her words came out like bullets. "I trusted you. And you betrayed me." As I stepped toward her, she moved backward, and suddenly I knew there was now a huge gulf of distrust and misunderstanding between us.

"I know you trusted me, Laine."

Tears formed in her eyes, threatening to break free. "This is horrible. Horrible." Her phone buzzed in the side pocket of her backpack and when she checked it, all the blood drained from her face. "Oh my God. They're texting the pic now, too."

"What?"

She showed me the screen, which had a message from Jillian that contained the photo and a few choice words. "This is the worst day of my life."

"Well, I don't know if it's the worst day—"

"Are you kidding me?" she shouted. She lowered her voice once she remembered the other students, who still stared at us. "You can't tell me it's not. I can't even . . . this is so horrible."

Of course it was horrible. Laine covered her face with her hand, as if she wanted to shut out the world, and the reality of the situation became clear to me. I was about to lose the only girl I'd ever cared about, the one girl I might really love. Over a fucking picture. I was going to lose her over a picture, and I hated Blake and Bruce so much at that moment. Those dimwits had won. Again. And after this fight, the whole school would know about it, and most people would laugh about it, and never let us forget it. Way to be the headline all around school.

"I'm sorry." She was slipping away from me, and I had no idea how to catch her again. "Geez, I'm so sorry for all the . . ."

"I'm sorry too, Geoff," She took another step backward, and this time I didn't try to follow her. She closed her eyes. "I can't do this."

"Can't do what?" I didn't want to ask this question, but I did it anyway.

"This. I can't do this."

"Us?" I whispered. "Can't do us?"

She turned her gaze to the floor. "Yeah. I can't do this. Not anymore. Not like this—with everything—this will never work, Geoff."

"Wait. It's not me. It's them—what about—you said—"

"I know what I said." She looked up from the floor, and I didn't see the tears any more. "But that was the wrong decision. I can't do this. Not like this."

I leaned my whole body up against the locker as the weight of what she was saying settled around me. She wanted to end this. She wanted to walk away from me. She didn't want me, not any more. Jesus *fucking* Christ.

"It's okay," I lied. "I understand. I get it."

"You're a nice guy, Geoff. I just can't do this." She paused. "Goodbye."

I opened my mouth to say something, but the bell

rang and stopped me. She gave me a sad smile, then turned and walked down the hallway. The few underclassmen around us sprang into action, too, scurrying to grab their notebooks, backpacks and iPads, and get to class for whatever final exams they had to complete that day. I stood alone against one of the lockers, and watched the hallway clear. All I needed to do was go to a couple of bullshit classes that morning, then take the AP European History test in the afternoon, my last AP test of the year. That test didn't even count for my final grade in that class, it would just determine if I received college credit for my pain and suffering.

I didn't care about getting college credit any more. It just seemed so stupid, like something I had spent so much time on because I had nothing better to do. And what did I have to show for it?

"Screw it," I said. I pulled myself against the locker. "I don't need this. I don't care anymore."

It was true. I didn't. I had spent twelve years of school trying to be the best in the class, focusing on grades and pushing myself to outdo everyone, only to find that high school was about so much more than competition and completion. I had wasted so much time wishing I were somewhere else, looking for a better life, not noticing I had chances for a pretty good one right in front of me. And now I had lost a huge part of that because my stepbrothers pulled some underhanded bullshit.

I shook my head a few times, took a deep breath, and found my center. Then I turned, walked out of the hallway, back down the steps, and out of Heritage. My high school career only had two days left, anyway. Fuck it.

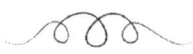

We'd buried my father in the hot, sweltering summer sun, on a Friday in July. After a long visitation and an even longer funeral, a black hearse led a caravan to Spring Grove Cemetery, a large and rambling historic site tucked in between the train tracks on the west side of downtown Cincinnati. Years later, all I remembered was how stifled and stiff the whole thing felt to me, like some kind of orchestrated event the adults in my life had planned because they didn't know what to do, or how to handle their grief.

At first, Mom and I visited Dad all the time. We drove to the cemetery on holidays and sometimes on weekends, and most of the time Mom brought flowers to place at the grave. I liked that she did it, and as a kid, I thought we'd always visit Dad.

By the time I started my senior year at Heritage, though, Mom didn't visit Dad with me anymore. She said it bothered her too much to make the drive over, and look at the sad little headstone that broke his life down to a name, date of birth, and date of death. She insisted time and time again that she didn't want to forget him, but she never talked about him anymore, either.

Life was funny like that. People told me they would remember my dad forever.

And then they forgot.

I drove to Spring Grove after I walked out of Heritage. I didn't really think about going there, I just did it, driving like a zombie until I parked the car in the cemetery parking lot and got out. Dad's grave was just a short walk from the main road, and while I could have driven right too it, I decided to walk. I needed the fresh air, and the clarity, something that the peaceful place of Spring Grove always brought me. Most of all, though, I needed my dad.

Maybe I'd been a total idiot to think Laine really liked me, or that it would ever work out between us. She didn't really know me, and all my Facebook stalking hadn't really left me knowing her, either. Who was I to think I deserved her?

I sat down on the grass once I got to Dad's grave. He rested underneath a small granite rectangle in the middle of a long, neat row of headstones. Flowers and mementos adorned almost every one of them.

I sat that way for a long time, just thinking. High school was basically over. I'd skipped my last AP test, and only one day of school stood between me, and graduation. I'd been dreaming of this day since seventh grade, the year I turned awkward instead of cool, first laid eyes on Laine Phillips, and heard the escalating taunts of my classmates. In less than two days, I'd be free of all of the past. After graduation, I didn't have to walk through the halls of Heritage ever again.

So why didn't I feel so great about that?

"Jesus Christ," I muttered, to no one but myself. "I need to pull my shit together."

I kept repeating that over and over until around eleven a.m., when the phone in my pocket buzzed. I pulled it out and saw a message from Josh.

11:01AM
Josh: *Are you okay? Just saw pic on Facebook. Laine left school.*

Me: *She skipped the AP test?*

Josh: *Yep. Walked out. Heard she was crying.*

Disgusted, I shoved the phone back in my pocket and stood up. I had a mission; I knew what I had to do. And nothing was going to stop me.

Nothing.

Laine's house looked creepy and imposing as I pulled up to it about a half hour later. On the drive over from Spring Grove, I stopped twice: once at a gas station, and once at a McDonald's, because I thought was going to throw up. She and I needed to talk, but I couldn't figure out what to say. More than ever, though, I needed to find the right words.

My nerves got even worse when I saw her car in the driveway. By the time I walked up to the door, sweat covered my hands, back and neck. Thank God I had a black shirt on, and she wouldn't be able to see it. I just hoped she couldn't smell it, as I wiped my hands on my jeans and rapped on the door.

Knock. Knock.

I waited. Three minutes passed. No answer.

Knock. Knock. Knock.

I waited some more.

She had to have heard me, because I had a strong knock. Jesus, waiting for her to answer was total agony. She hated me, and I knew it. Laine blamed me for so much, and she'd said as much in the hallway at school. She probably never wanted to talk to me again, but I didn't care. I was staying.

Knock. Knock. Knock.

The red door flew open a few seconds later. She stood behind it, scowling, with red-rimmed eyes that told me she'd been crying an ugly, deep cry. "What do you want?"

"Look, I'm sorry." I leaned forward a little, but I didn't walk inside. She hadn't invited me in, and I didn't know what to do so I just stood there, wavering, and wondering if I shouldn't have come over at all.

"Really, Laine. I'm sorry. I didn't know they would find that picture."

She leaned one hand against the door, and turned her head.

"I'm serious."

"It's all over Facebook," she said, still not looking at me. "It's everywhere."

"I know." I sucked in a breath. "Look, high school's over. It is. One more day of school. And then you can just move on."

She finally turned to me, and when she did, I saw a few more tears threaten to fall down her cheeks. "You don't get it, Geoff. It's not just that. It's not just the picture, it's the whole thing."

"The whole what?"

"I don't want people thinking I didn't care about Evan. I did. I really did. Even though he had problems, his faults. I loved him once, and now it looks like I never did. I don't want to do that to a dead guy's memory. That's just wrong. Really wrong."

"I'm sure no one thinks—"

She frowned at me. "No, you're wrong. They do. People said stuff to me about it in first period. They think I never cared about Evan at all." She paused. "They think I was cheating on him the whole time."

I almost laughed, but I choked it back. "I'm sure they don't think you were cheating on him with me."

"Of course they think that! You would, too, if you weren't with me." She scowled. "Aren't you always judging everyone, anyway?"

Her words stung, and I recoiled. She had a point. I'd spent all this time in high school judging people, and it had gotten me nowhere. All it caused was pain, and it made me miss out on the things each person had to offer. I should have told her that, but I didn't. I just gulped, and didn't say anything at all.

"Whatever. You don't get it." Her tone of voice made me want to shudder. Harsh. Cold. Indifferent. She'd never spoke to me like this before, as if she wished we'd never met. It crushed me. Wounded me. Hurt me, more than anything I had felt in a long time.

"I'm sorry you feel that way," I finally managed. "Really sorry."

"Just go, Geoff," she said, after another moment passed. "Please go."

I held my feelings inside until I stopped the car at the stop sign at the end of the street. That whole conversation hadn't gone the way I'd imagined it would, at all. What a disaster. I beat my fists against the steering wheel, and screamed a few times. Then I yelled a couple of choice words—most of which involved some version of the word "fuck." It didn't make me feel much better. Then, after a few seconds, I found the strength to drive home.

My bed had never seemed so comforting. I fell onto it, wrapped myself in the striped comforter, and fell asleep.

I woke up hours later, my brain still a foggy mess. At first, I thought maybe it hadn't happened. Maybe I hadn't skipped the AP test, lost the one girl I cared about, and become an Internet laughing stock all in one day. Maybe I'd been stuck in a nightmare, like one of those "After School Special" TV clichés.

But that didn't last for very long. Oh, no. My misery was real—too real, and I couldn't sleep it away, no matter how much I tried.

I glanced at my watch and saw it was almost four p.m. Holy shit. I bolted out of bed. Blake and Bruce would be home. Right then. I bet they were in the kitchen, eating huge snacks, pleased with themselves and totally unconcerned about what they did to me. They'd probably been home for a while, those assholes. I couldn't let them get away with this at all.

Confrontation time.

Stumbling down the stairs, I tried to gather my thoughts and figure out what I would say. Maybe I wouldn't say anything at all. Maybe I needed to just punch them. I could pretend like it never happened, and that might freak them out. Or I could start screaming just before I hit the kitchen, giving them fair warning that I was about to unleash a fury on them.

In the end, I kinda mixed a couple of ideas together. Something about hearing their laughter in the kitchen just sort of set me off. It hit me deep in my core, as if their laughter was some kind of veiled insult directed at me, and only me. Oh hell, no. They were not going to get away with this.

"Nice work guys," I said from the doorframe that linked the kitchen with the wide great room in the center of the house. Blake looked over at me, a popcorn-stuffed hand poised to hit his mouth. Bruce, on the other hand, took a calm sip of his Coke, and didn't even bother to glance in my direction.

"Really, good work," I continued. "Your best yet." I took a step inside the kitchen. "You know, I knew you guys had a problem with me, but I didn't know you hated me this much."

Bruce snickered.

Blake stuffed the popcorn into his mouth and chewed, as if whatever I was saying didn't bother him in the least. "Who says we hate you?" he said, giving me a full view of the food in his mouth. "We don't hate you, dear brother."

"Whatever," Bruce added, as if he were talking to a small child who needed extra help understanding something. "What would make you think we hated you now?"

"I saw the flyers." I struggled to keep myself steady as my hands formed two fists at my sides. They knew full well what I was referring to. I knew they did; there was no way they couldn't. "I know what you did. Nice work on going through my iPhone, and then sharing it with everyone."

"Oh, that," Blake said calmly. "Right. Well. Someone had to point it out. Your fault that you didn't lock up your phone. Shoulda' done that one."

"Oh, really?" I heard and felt my anger rising with each ticking second. "You want to blame me for this? You guys knew what you were doing. You wanted to make me look like an idiot, and ruin my life."

"We did not ruin your sad little life," Blake said. "So stop being such a dramatic prick."

"I'm not being a dramatic prick." I crossed the room until I stood right next to the chair where Blake sat. "I'm not. You're the assholes! All I have ever done is try to help you. I've been nice to you. I've left you alone. And all you do is treat me like you hate me."

"Everyone hates you, Geoff." Blake's calm tone didn't match my urgent one, and that made me even madder.

"I'm so sick—I'm so sick of—I'm so sick of you!" I yelled.

And that's when I punched him.

My right fist landed with a crack on the bridge of his nose. The cartilage snapped and creaked as my fist made contact, and for a split second I had the upper hand as I pulled back, then hit his face again, this time in the left eye. By the time I pulled back a third time, though, Bruce had jumped out of his seat, and he grabbed my arm as I prepared to send my fist colliding with Blake's face. As Bruce restrained me, a now bloody Blake sailed his fist into my stomach, then my jaw, my nose, and finally his right cross slammed into my left eye.

"Let me go," I shouted as his fist made contact. I struggled against Bruce's tight grip as Blake's fist met my stomach again. "Ooof. Let me fucking go, assholes."

"I hate you," Blake said. I crumpled up against his brother, and doubled over in pain. "You're like a symbol of everything that's wrong with our lives. Mr. Perfect: the asshole."

"I'm not perfect," I mumbled, and as I did blood started to drip down my nose. "Far from it."

"Oh yeah?"

"Yeah. I've been wrong about a lot of stuff."

"Maybe we should stop," Bruce said to his brother. "He's pretty bloody, and so are you."

Out of the corner of my eye I saw Blake wipe some blood off his nose. "Fine," he said. "Fine. I think he gave me a black eye, anyway."

Once Bruce released me, I made sure I looked them booth in the eye, swallowing any fear I had, and turning all my emotions into anger. "Don't ever threaten me again," I said in the strongest voice I had. "Don't ever talk to me like I'm less than again. Ever. Leave me the fuck alone, and I'll do the same with you. Got it?"

As soon as they nodded in agreement, I turned and walked out of the room.

Chapter seventeen

FRIDAY, MAY 17TH

WHEN I DIDN'T come downstairs for breakfast, Mom brought breakfast to me. She walked up the stairs with a bagel and glass of orange juice to find me still in bed. The last day of high school had finally come, but I couldn't bring myself to get up and even try to act like I cared.

"You're not going, honey?" She said when I didn't get up from the bed.

"Nope, I'm not." I'd been awake for about thirty minutes. My clothes lay draped and untouched over the chair at my desk, and my book bag rested in a heap beneath them. They disgusted me, and so did my eye, which throbbed.

Blake had a great right cross. I needed to remember that for next time.

"But what about—"

"What does it matter, Mom? I don't have any exams today. And it's not like we're doing anything but practicing for graduation."

She put the food on the desk, tightened her robe, and took a seat at the edge of my bed. "That eye of yours is really coming in. You'll have a nice shiner for the ceremony tomorrow."

"I don't care." Then I bit back a smile. "Does Blake's eye still look bad, too?"

"It does. The bruise is pretty big." She bit back a smile. "And his nose doesn't look so great, either."

"Good." I didn't even try to hide my delight. I gave him what he deserved. Well, he really deserved more than that, but maybe my punch had sent a message. "Maybe he'll remember for next time."

"I don't like to hear about you guys fighting like that." She sighed. "It's really hard for me, you know, to always know what to do."

"They're assholes. Jerks."

"They don't always treat you very well. You're right about that."

I sighed, exasperated. "Mom, they hacked into my phone, looked through my personal photos, found one of me with Laine, and shared it with everyone!"

"I know. David and I discussed it with them."

"You did?" I sat up in bed, adjusting myself against the fluffy pillows. I didn't take my eyes off of her. I needed her to answer this question.

"We did. They know it was unacceptable." She scooted closer to me. "We've made that very clear. Both of them had their allowance cut."

"They did?" I said, unable to hide my surprise. "Good."

"You sound shocked, honey."

"Just didn't expect that. That was bullshit what they did," I muttered. "Total bullshit." I didn't need to add that it might have singlehandedly ruined my love life.

"You know I hate it when you cuss, Geoff." She sounded more half-hearted than upset.

"Well, that's the best word for this," I said. Then the bagel caught my eye. She had fixed it just the way I liked, toasted with honey nut cream cheese. "Thanks for the breakfast."

She got up, grabbed the plate and the glass from the desk, and handed them to me. I gulped down some of the juice and took an eager bite into the bagel. She watched me, a half amused expression on her face.

"You know, I'm really proud that you're going to be salutatorian," she said, once I'd eaten about half of the bagel. "That's pretty awesome. More than awesome. What an accomplishment. And you're going to UVA. That's even better."

"I still haven't figured out what I want to major in," I told her, after I swallowed. "I've been thinking about it a lot, but I can't decide."

"You don't have to decide right now." A wistful smile came over her face. "Have you thought about your speech for tomorrow?"

"No," I admitted. "That's what I want to do today, while I stay home."

She cocked her head. "So I can't convince you to go back to Heritage one more time? Just once more?"

I shook my head.

"I guess I don't blame you. I wouldn't want to go either." She stood up from the bed and walked to the doorframe. Then she turned around. "You know, Geoff, I really do love you. And I'm sorry if you haven't felt that way in a while."

"I love you, too, Mom."

About fifteen minutes after she left, still in my boxer shorts and T-shirt, I turned on the computer. I had one more thing to do before I could leave high school behind and never think about my life there again. I had to get through my graduation speech.

And graduation.

SATURDAY, MAY 18

NO MATTER WHERE you were in America, high school graduation ceremonies were all pretty much the same: plenty of tears, lots of photos, and kids hugging and hanging onto each other, while they proclaimed they would always stay in touch.

David grunted as he slid the BMW into a parking spot in the church parking lot across the street from school. At his request, I'd ridden with him and Mom to the ceremony, and the twins caught a ride with their mom, Caroline. "I want to talk to you a minute, Geoff."

"Okay," I replied as David motioned for Mom to hop out of the car. Once she shut the door, he braced his hands on the wheel. "Is everything okay?"

"It's just fine," he said, looking at me through the rear-view mirror. "I just haven't found the time to say something to you that I wanted to say." He paused. "I'm very proud of the person you are becoming, Geoff."

I swallowed, and sank further into the leather seat.

"You are?"

"Yes." He took his hands off the wheel and turned to me a little. "You've done a lot of growing this year. Of course, your grades are outstanding. But it's the other stuff."

"I thought you hated me. Didn't want me around."

He sighed. "I didn't know how to handle another teenage boy." He gestured with one hand to the twins and their mother, who by then had met up with Mom in the parking lot. They all stood about ten feet away from the car, waiting for us to get out. "And you know I have my hands full with those two."

I laughed.

"Nice shiner on Blake, by the way," David said.

"I was mad."

"You've been mad for a long time, haven't you?" His voice had turned warmer. "I know you miss your dad. And that you sometimes feel out of place at school."

Wow. He'd been noticing a lot about me. More than I had expected.

"I'm glad I get to leave Robert Hill soon," I admitted, my eyes following the sea of students in graduation gowns, and parents with cameras. "Get to start my life. My real life."

"It's already started." David pulled the keys out of the car and opened the driver side door. "And you have a big speech to make." With one foot on the pavement, he looked back at me. "Just make your mother proud. And me."

"I will," I said as I opened my car door, too.

As we walked toward school, the twins acted like they might have been celebrities. They kept stopping to take photos with anyone they could find, even classmates of ours I knew they didn't like. It was funny to watch them, since they both had signature poses they did over and over again for each photo. They would have thought of something like that. It was just their kind of obnoxious style. I felt a twinge of jealousy, though, because one thing was obvious: the rest of my classmates would miss the twins.

I couldn't say the same for myself.

"Well," Mom said when we all arrived at Heritage's front entrance, "I guess we'll let you all get ready from here." She nodded in the direction of a clump of students headed to the side entrance of the school auditorium.

"I love you, Mom." I gave her a hug, and she held onto me tighter than normal.

"I love you too, Geoff," she whispered in my ear. "And make this speech count."

"Mr. Miller," Mr. Langston said behind me. When I whirled around, I saw that, for once, his shirt didn't have any food stains on it, and looked ironed. *Impressive.* "I just want you to know—we missed you in the AP test Thursday." He turned his attention to my mom. "I proctored the exam."

"I know I missed it," I said, but I wasn't apologizing. Not at all. "I just had some things to take care of—some stuff I needed to sort out."

"Well, I'm disappointed you won't be getting the college credit. Such a shame to study so hard and do so much work for nothing."

"I don't think it was for nothing," Mom spoke up. "I think Geoff has just learned a couple of things in the last few months. For one, there is more to life than a test."

"But surely, you think—"

"Geoff made the right decision for himself. There'll be other tests. Plenty of them, since he's going to study pre-law at Virginia."

I bit back a grin. Maybe she did understand me a little bit, after all.

Mr. Langston didn't look convinced, though. He still had a withered, disapproving look on his face. "You also missed the graduation ceremony prep from yesterday, Geoff."

"I know," I replied. "But I think I can figure out how it goes."

"I just think it's a shame that you—"

"Seniors," Mr. Henderson called. "It's time to make your way to the side hallway for the procession of the class."

Mr. Langston stepped aside. "Don't let me keep you, Mr. Miller."

As was tradition, all the seniors lined up in a row according to class rank, as we got ready to enter the stage. I tried to find Laine, but I couldn't pick her out of the line of red caps. Annoyed, I made my way to the line and grabbed a spot behind Nichole. She already had her cap on, and clutched her speech in her hand.

"So, are you ready?" she asked in her nasally voice.

"As ready as I'll ever be." I patted my pants underneath my robe. "Got my speech right here."

"I know we've been in competition these last few years," Nichole said, "but I just want you to know, I wouldn't want the salutatorian to be anyone else, but you."

"Thanks," I said as Mr. Henderson clapped his hands. This was Nichole's awkward way of giving me a compliment. "Good luck with your speech, Nichole."

Mr. Henderson clapped his hands together once more, shouted at us to be quiet, and the underclassmen in the high school band began to play the song for our processional into the school auditorium.

We all took spots on the stage, and then one of the juniors sang the national anthem in a warbling, breathy voice. Nichole and I sat in front, away from the rest of our classmates, next to Mayor Harris and the podium. Mr. Harris said a boring prayer, and then someone I didn't recognize who played with the Cincinnati Bengals gave a speech about following dreams, and achieving goals. A couple of times I had to stifle a chuckle when I glanced at Nichole, who seemed to grow more nervous with every second that passed.

Everyone knew she hated public speaking. This girl did everything right, but public speaking made her terrified. For me, on the other hand, public speaking was a total turn on, and I loved it. That's how I knew I was going to make a decent lawyer. When I wanted to, I could make quite a show. And, as was tradition, the salutatorian speech came first during the ceremony.

Even so, when Mayor Harris introduced me, a jolt went through my body. I'd given plenty of speeches in the past, but this one really counted. This one was the moment. There would be no turning back after this speech.

"Ladies and gentlemen, please welcome your class salutatorian, Geoff Miller, to the stage."

My classmates broke out into polite applause, which the audience of about four hundred echoed. I couldn't really see them, though, as I walked up to the podium. The glare of the lights blinded me as I unfolded my speech.

I cleared my throat. The microphone buzzed. "Good afternoon parents, teachers, and distinguished guests."

The applause from the crowd died down as I made sure to follow the rules of public speaking. Look up and address your audience. Relax the shoulders. Speak slowly. Vary tone of voice.

So why had my hands gone clammy, all of a sudden?

"We've spent twelve years trying to make it to this moment, and now we are finally here. This is the moment where we all stand on the edge of a new reality, a new freedom. But what does that mean?

"Socrates said . . ." I trailed off, and looked at the pages. The word blurred and twisted, so I shut my eyes and shook my head. When I opened them, it still wasn't better. The five pages of my speech contained all kinds of highbrow literary quotes, and advice about life that could have been off of the *Dr. Phil* show. It had all sounded so good the night before when I'd read it aloud ten times, and performed it in front of the mirror. Now, it just sounded like something an asshole with no concept of what he really wanted to say would use as a crutch.

Oh, no, this wouldn't work. It wouldn't work at all.

I didn't hesitate. I picked the speech up from the podium, crumpled it up in a ball, and tossed if offstage. It was time to man up, for the four thousandth time in my life.

"Let me just be honest right now," I told the audience. "That speech sucked. It wasn't right. I thought it was, but it wasn't. It didn't even come close to what I want to say."

I swallowed. "Most of you know my name is Geoff Miller, and I've spent the last few years overachieving at Heritage while I competed for grades, and tried to be the best. Only today, I'm second best." I raised my hand to Nichole, whose eyes had widened. "I hated you for it for a long time, Nichole, and I'm sorry about that. You won. You deserved to win. You're smart and driven, confident and pretty. You make a great valedictorian, and I mean it when I say congratulations."

The crowd broke out in faint unsure applause. I should have waited for them to finish before I started up again, but I didn't.

Onward.

"I've been miserable for most of high school. Jealous. Envious. I wanted what others had, and since I couldn't get it, I wanted to get out of here as soon as possible. Robert Hill wasn't for me, and I decided that long ago."

I turned to my classmates. "What I wasn't seeing, though, was that along the way, I had met some really good guys—some real friends. Josh, Nathan, and Mark, I'm sorry if I didn't appreciate you. You guys have stood by me and been there for me this whole time, but I've never stopped and said how much it means to me. But maybe I didn't realize it until this weekend. Most people wait their whole lives to have good friends who challenge them, and make them better every day. For twelve years, you've done that to me. So thank you."

I cocked my head as I turned back to the crowd. I considered where I wanted to go next with my words. Then, suddenly, I knew.

"I almost missed something else during my last year

here at Heritage, something even more important than friendship." My face flushed, but I continued anyway. "I almost missed out on love.

"I'm not talking about romantic love—not really. I almost missed out on a girl, who showed me what it meant to love others, and to care. Laine Phillips. These last six months have been so much better because she's been in my life." I looked back at my classmates on the stage, and finally locked eyes with her, where she sat, at the far end of the second row. "A lot of people in life have told Laine she's perfect. In fact, some people make fun of her for being that way, like a perfect princess.

"I know she's not perfect. No one is. But I also know this—Laine is a good person. She loves other people. She cares about other people." I swallowed again, my mouth running drier with each second that passed. "She cared about Evan Carpenter. She might have even loved him, in the real way that is something special and unique between two people.

"Now, I'm not here to speak badly about a person, and certainly not about a dead person, but, ladies and gentlemen, I need for you to know this: Evan Carpenter didn't treat Laine very well—at least, not the way he should have, at the end of his life. And that's the bare truth.

"Somehow, this kind and funny girl let me get to know her these last few months, and I'll tell anyone it was pretty amazing. She made me—well, she made me a better person. She helped me see what I've been missing this whole time, while I've hated my life at Heritage, and judging everyone around me. I've been missing out on a chance to be around people for a moment in time that changes us all.

"High school isn't forever. It's four awkward years, which, when you really think about it, isn't that long of life at all. But the thing about these four years is that, if you let yourself, you get to see people become the adults they are going to be. You get to see your classmates and friends come into their own.

"I almost didn't, though. I shut myself away, angry, because I thought you guys all had judged me as someone I wasn't. But maybe you all hadn't. She didn't." I gulped. "Just two days ago, though, I lost Laine. I did something stupid, and it came back to haunt me. Some people manipulated an innocent picture and made it look like more than it really was, just so they could get at me.

"Laine, I'm sorry. I'm really sorry. I'm also sorry those same people and I could never get along. That we missed our chance to be brothers."

With a nod at Blake and Bruce, I turned back to the crowd.

"These speeches are always supposed to be about the future. They're supposed to inspire, command, and push us all into a world that awaits us. I know I'm supposed to stand up here and act like I have all the answers, as if being ranked second in the class makes me one of the kids who knows everything. But I don't. Not really. I don't know what the future is going to bring, and I don't know how things will turn out for any of us. This last year alone, I changed my major four times, and I haven't even started classes at UVA. Right now I want to be a lawyer, but next week I might want to be a stockbroker. Or a teacher. Or I might want to quit school all together, and travel the world with a backpack and sandals. I don't know."

I paused and took a sip of water from the bottle underneath the podium. "And that's okay. It's okay that I don't know what the future is going to bring. I don't think anyone in here really does. The fact is, all I really know is that I got an undeniably good education here at Heritage High School. Robert Hill's schools are some of the best in the area for a reason. I know it. Everyone on this stage knows it. And for that, I'm thankful. School here was hard on a lot of levels for me, but I think college will be easier because of this place. I hope I leave here a better person, because I think that's the most important thing in life: to grow from each experience. So. That's my message. Thank you. That's all I can really say. Thank you."

I waited for about five seconds to try and gauge the audience reaction, but there wasn't much of one until I stepped away from the podium. Once I did, a tepid applause broke out from the audience, noise that grew louder with each clap. I grinned once I got to my seat, relieved. I'd done it. I'd spoken from the heart. And that's what counted the most.

"Nice speech, son," Mayor Harris said, over Nichole's shoulder.

"I know. It really was." Nichole looked from me, to the mayor, and back again. "How am I supposed to follow that up?"

I shrugged, a grin still spread across my face. The truth was, I barely even noticed Nichole any more. I was too busy looking past her, at the end of the second row. Laine held my attention, because she was staring right at me, but I couldn't read her expression. Did she hate me for what I said? Had I embarrassed her? Where did my words leave us?

"I love you," I mouthed to her. I didn't even try to

stop myself. Not this time. I'd already come this far, and might as well go the whole way. I did love her, and I knew it at that moment. Even if she never wanted anything else to do with me, if she never looked my way again, I loved her. Laine Phillips had been the one thing that propelled me through senior year, and every cell in my body knew that. This wasn't lust, or sex, or a random hookup at all. What I felt for her was love.

Nichole stood up as the applause died down, but again, I only saw her do this with my peripheral vision. I still had my eye on the girl I loved. And after what could have been a thousand heartbeats, Laine smiled.

She smiled right at me.

The rest of graduation passed in a blur. Of course, just to be polite, I did turn my head back to the front and listened to Nichole's speech, but to be honest, I didn't hear a word of what she said. Walking across the stage and grabbing my diploma became a foggy memory, too, even as I did it. I heard my name, of course, and I took the rolled up diploma from Mr. Langston's hands, but I didn't really remember that, either.

All I thought about was Laine, and her smile. She'd smiled at me. And that was enough.

Well, at least for right then.

After the ceremony my mom fished me out of the crowd, and forced me to pose for more photos with Blake and Bruce. They still weren't speaking to me, but the finality of graduation must have put them in a charitable mood, because they didn't protest as Mom posed us for photos on the stage, by the standing flag poles, next to the mural of the school seal, and outside the building with Heritage's gothic glory posed artfully behind us. It didn't matter that the crowds of crying students, proud parents, and curious well-known citizens blocked us from getting perfect photos. She directed us with a precision Steven Spielberg would envy, and for once, all of us just allowed her to do it without protesting.

She'd just taken the fifth photo of the three of us next to some of the landscaping when I felt a tug on the loose fabric of my graduation gown. I saw Mom's smile get bigger, so I knew who it was before I turned around. Even so, my heart grew a few sizes when I saw Laine standing there, next to the large oak tree in the front of the school.

"Hey," I said. Because, you know, that's what you say to the girl you love. Something smooth. Like hey.

"Hey." She grinned. "Is that all?"

"So." I took a step closer to her, so we both stood underneath the tree. "I hope it was okay, what I said during that speech."

"Well, if I thought I didn't have any secrets before, I certainly don't have them now."

"I just needed to say that. I couldn't let the moment get away from me."

She glanced down at her black high-heeled pumps. "Sure. It came from the heart, didn't it?"

"Well, I had a better senior year because of you." I paused. "I meant that."

"You did?"

I propped my hand against the tree right next to her head, and leaned in a little. "Yeah. I meant that." I gestured back to my family, who, for all I knew stood about ten feet away, staring at us. "I spent too much time here hating stuff, and I didn't realize I was missing out on just about everything."

"I way overreacted earlier this week. I did." She blushed. "I didn't know what to do, so I just shut down."

"It's okay. It was a stupid prank. Bruce and Blake are idiots. I think they have mashed potatoes for brains."

"Nice damage on Bruce. I'm guessing you did that?"

"Oh, sure, and he gave me this." I pointed to my eye. "But it's whatever."

She laughed, and after a beat, I did, too.

Even though the red graduation gown swallowed her, there wasn't a prettier girl on the lawn at that second, and that wasn't because of Laine's physical looks. It was because of the way her spirit flowed out of her. She had that something—that unforgettable charisma. Just being around it felt like being home. We might as well have been the only people on the lawn right then. I didn't care about anyone or anything else.

"Did you mean what you said?"

"What? During the speech?"

She put her hand on my shoulder. "No, silly. After. When you sat down."

I gave her a mock frown. "Hmm. What did I say?"

"You said you loved me. Did you mean it?" She grinned. "Or were you just trying to save my reputation, in some epic way?"

"Well, sometimes princesses need saving." I sucked in a deep breath. "And I meant it. I love you, Laine."

Now she broke into a wider grin, which painted her face. "Princess. There's that nickname again."

"It's not a nickname. It's the truth."

"I love you, too, Geoff. I do."

She stopped talking because my lips were on hers. I didn't care about the crowd, or what people might see. I didn't care if they gawked. I kissed her with force, pushing her against the tree so hard that when I pulled away, she sucked in a long deep breath as her face flushed. "I love you like I've never loved anyone else."

"Good. Because otherwise I've made a pretty huge mistake with that speech back there."

She laughed. "But what are we going to do about it? You're going to UVA next year, and I'm going to Xavier."

"I know." I pursed my lips.

"I hate this. I wish—I wish I had figured this out sooner."

"We'll figure it out," I replied, confident. I kissed her again, this time a lot faster, but no less passionate. "We'll make it work."

"You think so?" Her lips hovered above mine.

"I know so."

She nuzzled her face in the crook of my shoulder, still smiling. "Wow. Well. I always wanted to find a Prince Charming." She looked up at me. "I just didn't think Prince Charming would be you."

My hand caught her chin. "Of course I'm Prince Charming. And I've been here all along."

Sometimes, fairy tales really do happen. Even to guys. I know, because one happened to me.

ACKNOWLEDGMENTS

TO THE READERS of this book, thank you so much. I'm so happy to have a chance to share Geoff's story with you.

This work would never have been possible without the amazing support of some awesome people. I'm in awe of how many people have helped me on this never-ending writing journey.

To my husband, Sean: every day I am so grateful for you. You make this life possible, and I can't thank you enough. I love you more than you could ever know.

To my beta readers, thank you from the bottom of my heart. Tasia, Jamie, Lisa, Cynthia, and Amy, your feedback was especially critical in making this story the best it could be as I edited it. Thank you for your enthusiasm, kind words, and encouragement.

To Lauren McKellar, my editor, a huge thank you as well. You rock. You pushed this story to new heights.

Thank you to Mayhem Cover Creations for the superb book cover design, and to Amy Elisabeth Photography and Joel Geiman for the photo. What an unforgettable cover shoot day! You all saw my vision, and created just what this book needed.

To the members of The Celi Circle, much love to each of you. The excitement, joy, and thrill you each seem to get from my writing keeps me doing this. I don't know what I would do without you all!

ABOUT THE AUTHOR

NEW ORLEANS BORN, S. Celi has lived all over the United States. She calls the Greater Cincinnati area and the Queen City home. She has spent more than a decade of her life working in journalism. She graduated cum laude from Western Kentucky University in 2004.

In her spare time, she likes to read, shop, write, travel, run long distances, volunteer with the Junior League, and fundraise for Cooperative for Education, a non-profit providing educational opportunities for Guatemalan kids.

For more information about S. Celi and her books, visit:

https://www.facebook.com/pages/Sara-Celi/252615174437
http://www.saraceli.com/
http://celibrationoflife.wordpress.com/
https://twitter.com/SaraGCeli

Other Works by S. Celi

The Palms
The Undesirable

Made in the USA
Charleston, SC
24 June 2014